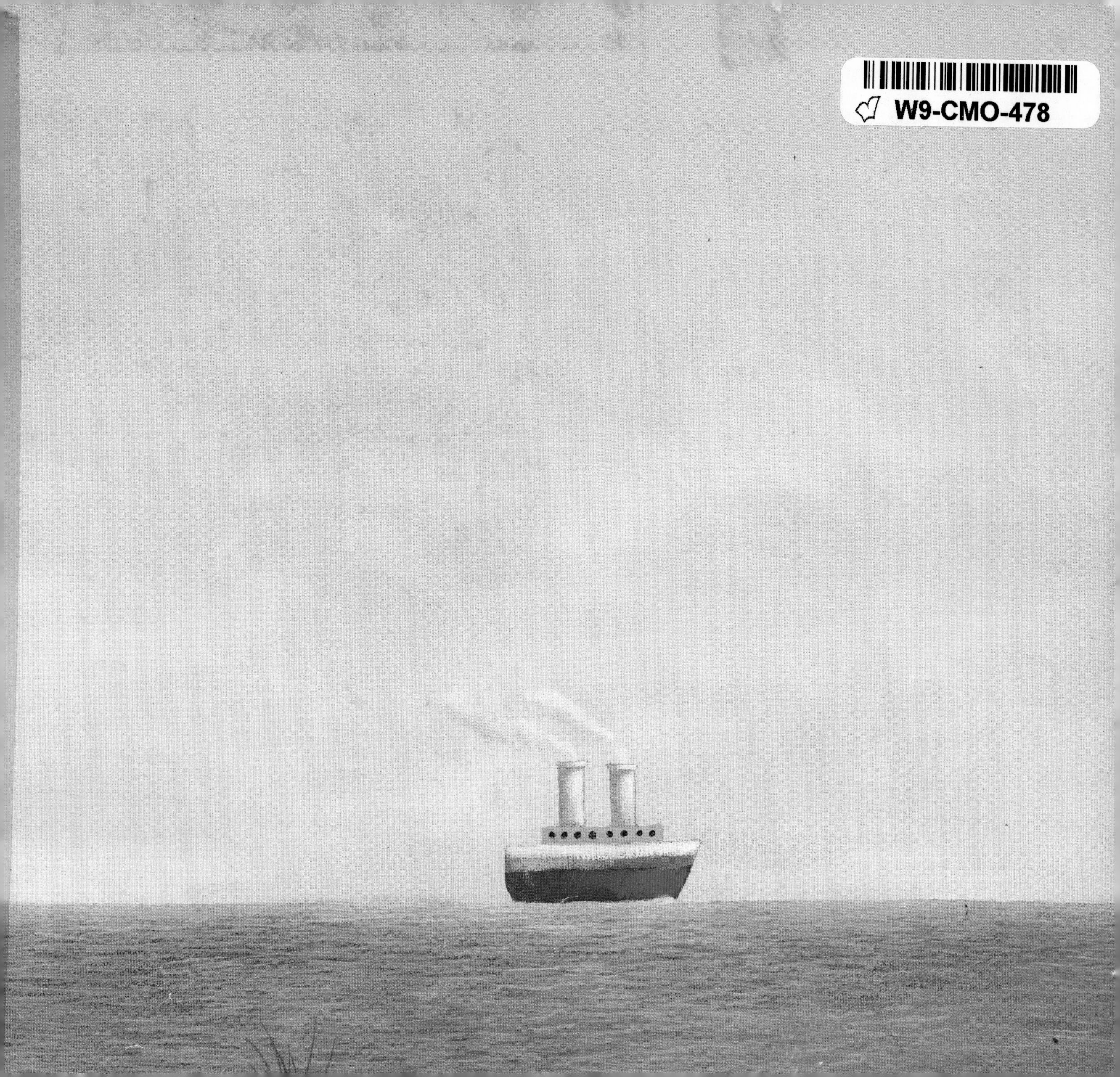

All rights reserved. Published in the United States by Random House Children's Books,
a division of Random House, Inc., New York.

Random House and the colophon are registered trademarks of Random House, Inc.

Visit us on the Web! randomhouse.com/kids

Educators and librarians, for a variety of teaching tools,
visit us at RHTeachersLibrarians.com

michaelparaskevas.com

Library of Congress Cataloging-in-Publication Data
Paraskevas, Michael.
Taffy Saltwater's yummy summer day / written and illustrated by Michael Paraskevas.
— 1st ed.
    p.   cm.
Summary: Taffy and her friends' plan to build the perfect sandcastle is interrupted
when Rollo the beach ball is blown away by an errant breeze.
ISBN 978-0-307-97892-9 (trade) — ISBN 978-0-375-97130-3 (lib. bdg.) —
ISBN 978-0-375-98125-8 (ebook)
[1. Friendship—Fiction. 2. Beaches—Fiction. 3. Sandcastles—Fiction.] I. Title.
PZ7.P21352Taf 2013 [E]—dc23 2012039109

MANUFACTURED IN CHINA
10 9 8 7 6 5 4 3 2 1
First Edition

*For Betty,
who taught me to love the
boardwalks of New Jersey*

Taffy Saltwater's Yummy Summer Day

Michael Paraskevas

Random House 🏠 New York

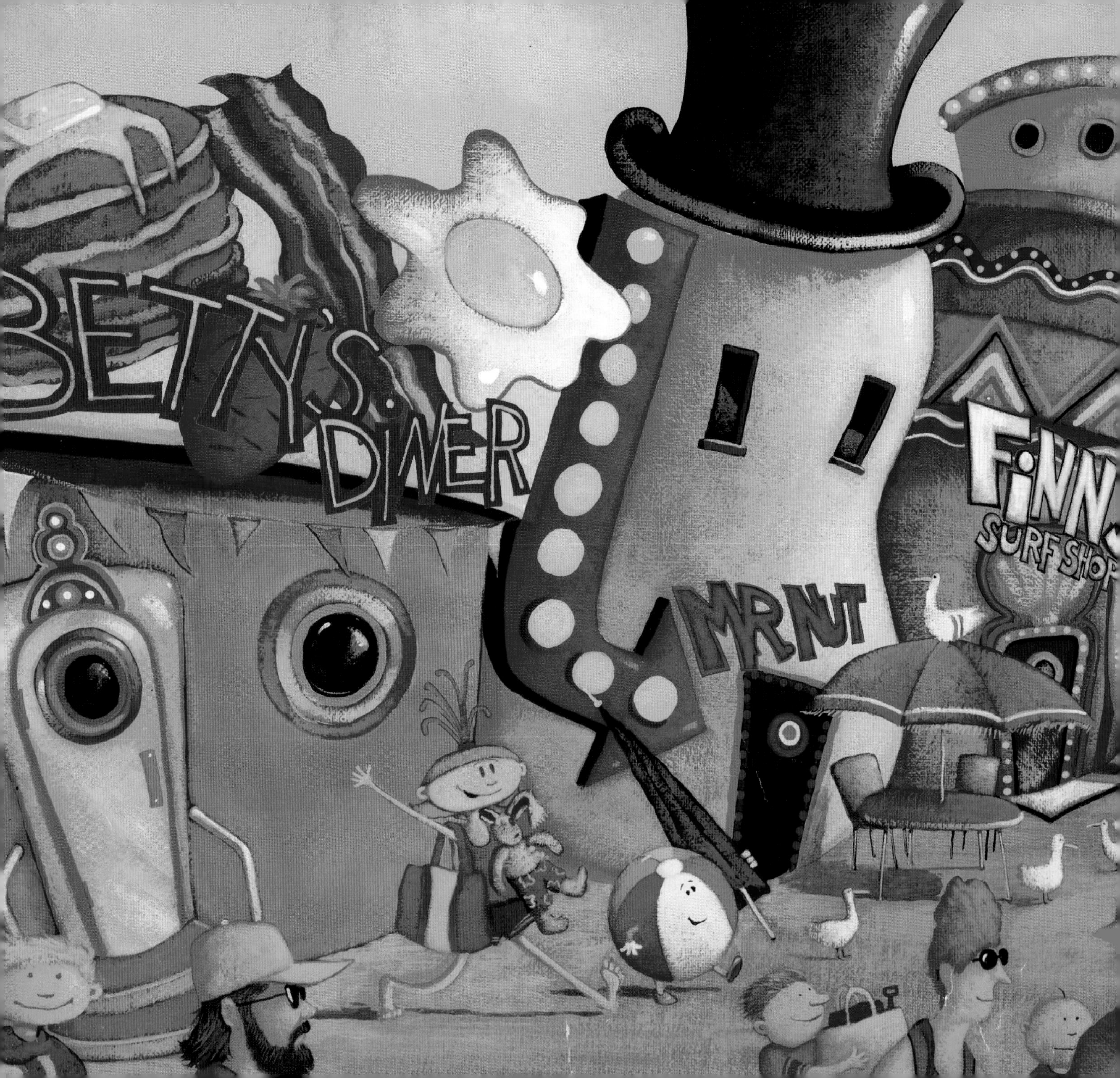
BETTY'S DINER
MR NUT
FINN'S
SURF SHOP

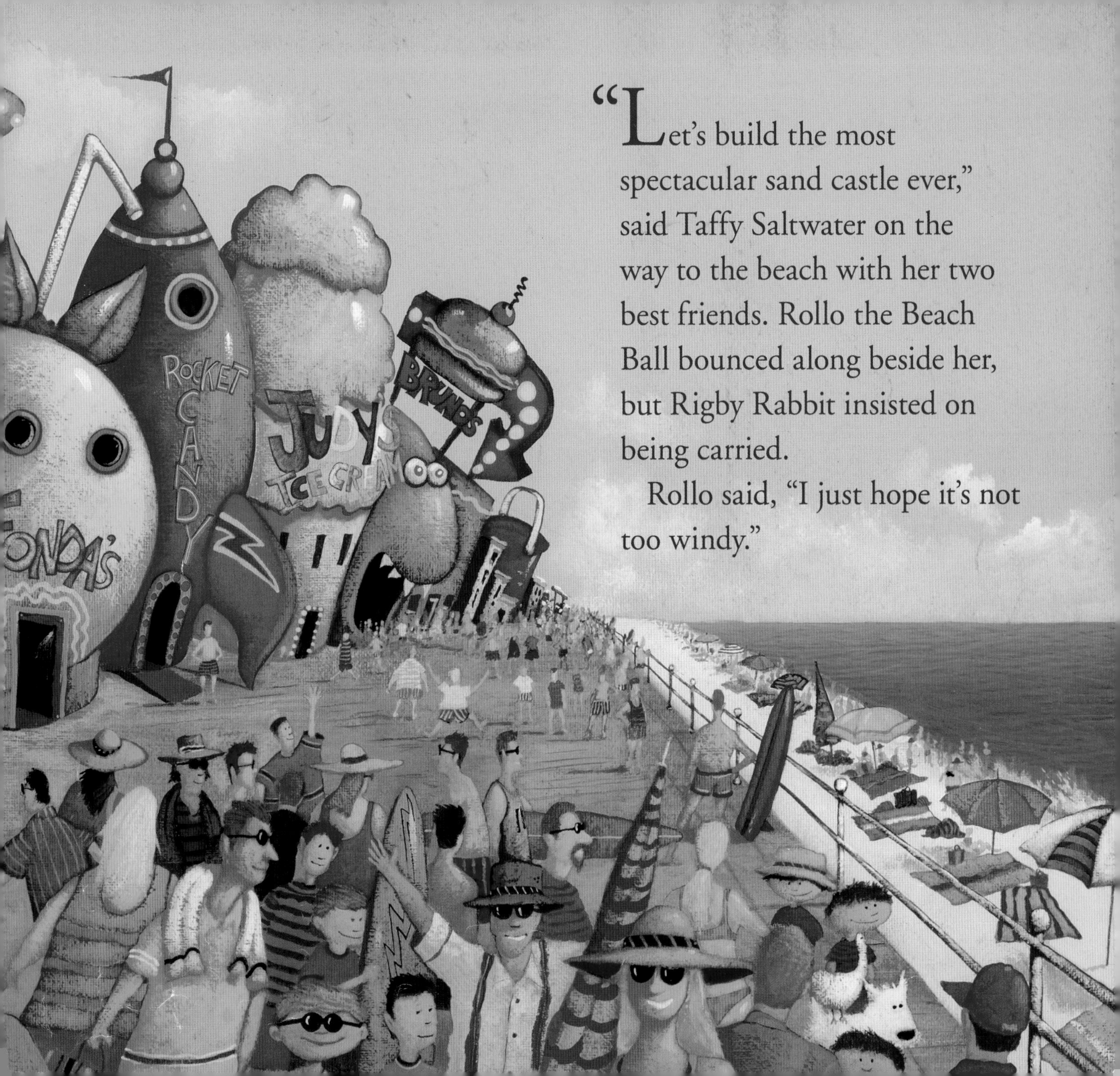
ROCKET CANDY
JUDYS
ICE CREAM
BRUNOS

"Let's build the most spectacular sand castle ever," said Taffy Saltwater on the way to the beach with her two best friends. Rollo the Beach Ball bounced along beside her, but Rigby Rabbit insisted on being carried.

Rollo said, "I just hope it's not too windy."

They crossed the boardwalk, where the wonderful smell of hot dogs, the music of the carousel and the warm sun all mixed with the salty beach air.

Taffy waved to Mr. Footer the Hot Dog Man, Edna the Lemon-Ice Lady and Chris the Lifeguard.

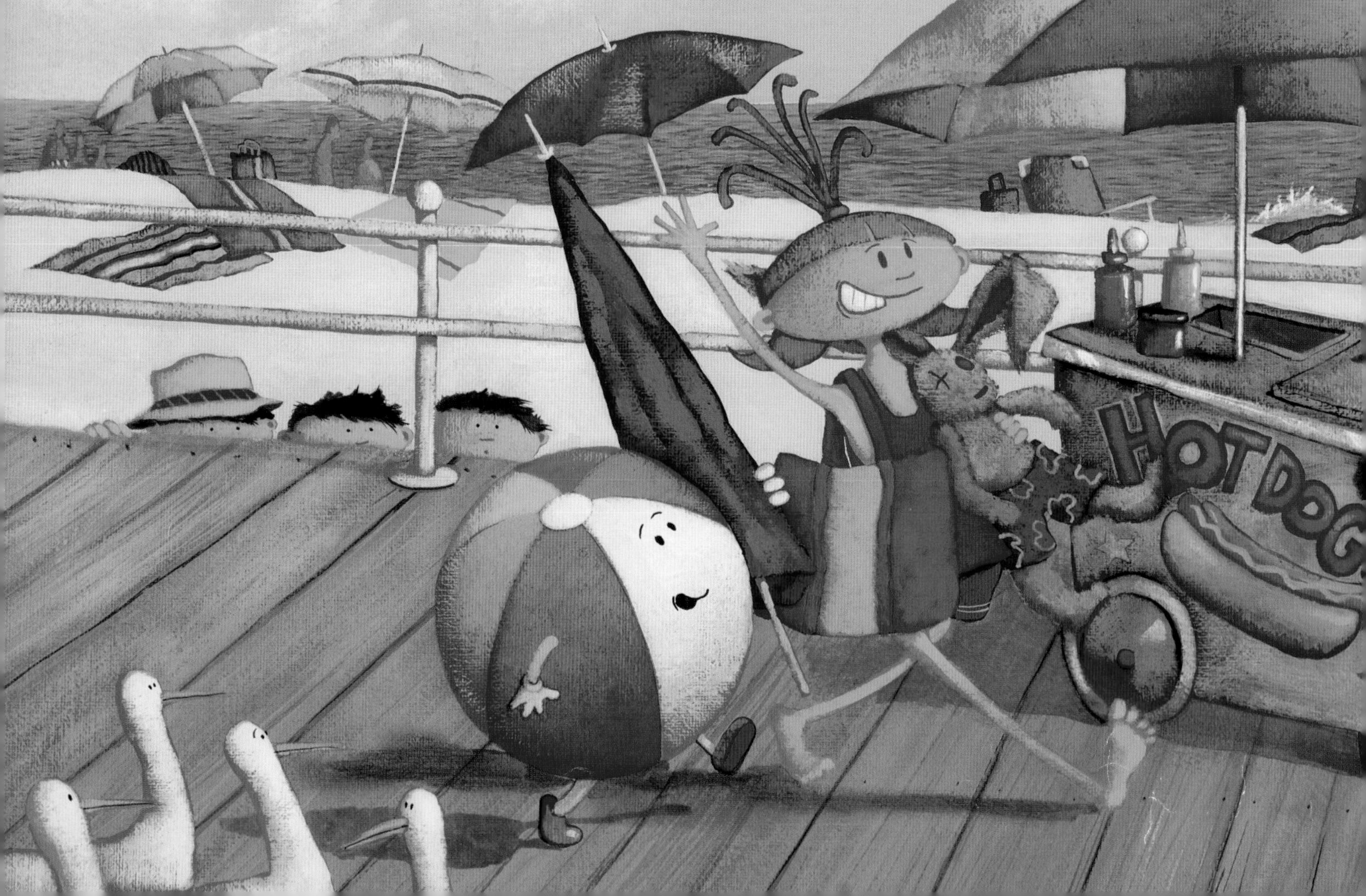
HOT DOG

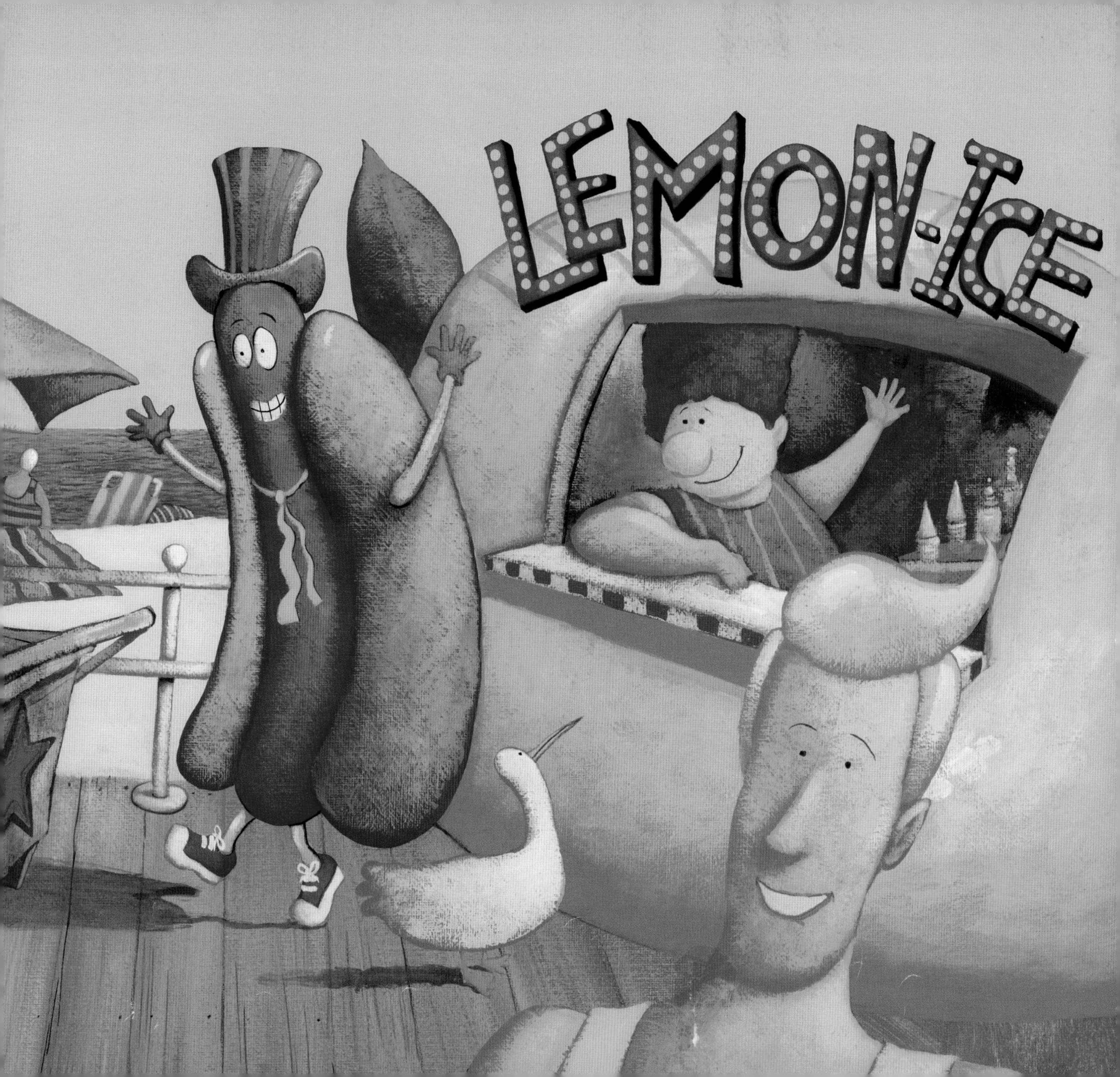
LEMON-ICE

Rigby didn't like the beach. "It's too hot. The sand gets in my furry feet. There's nothing to do."

"We forgot Bob," said Taffy.

She reached into her bag, pulled out Bob the Sea Monster and began pumping him full of air.

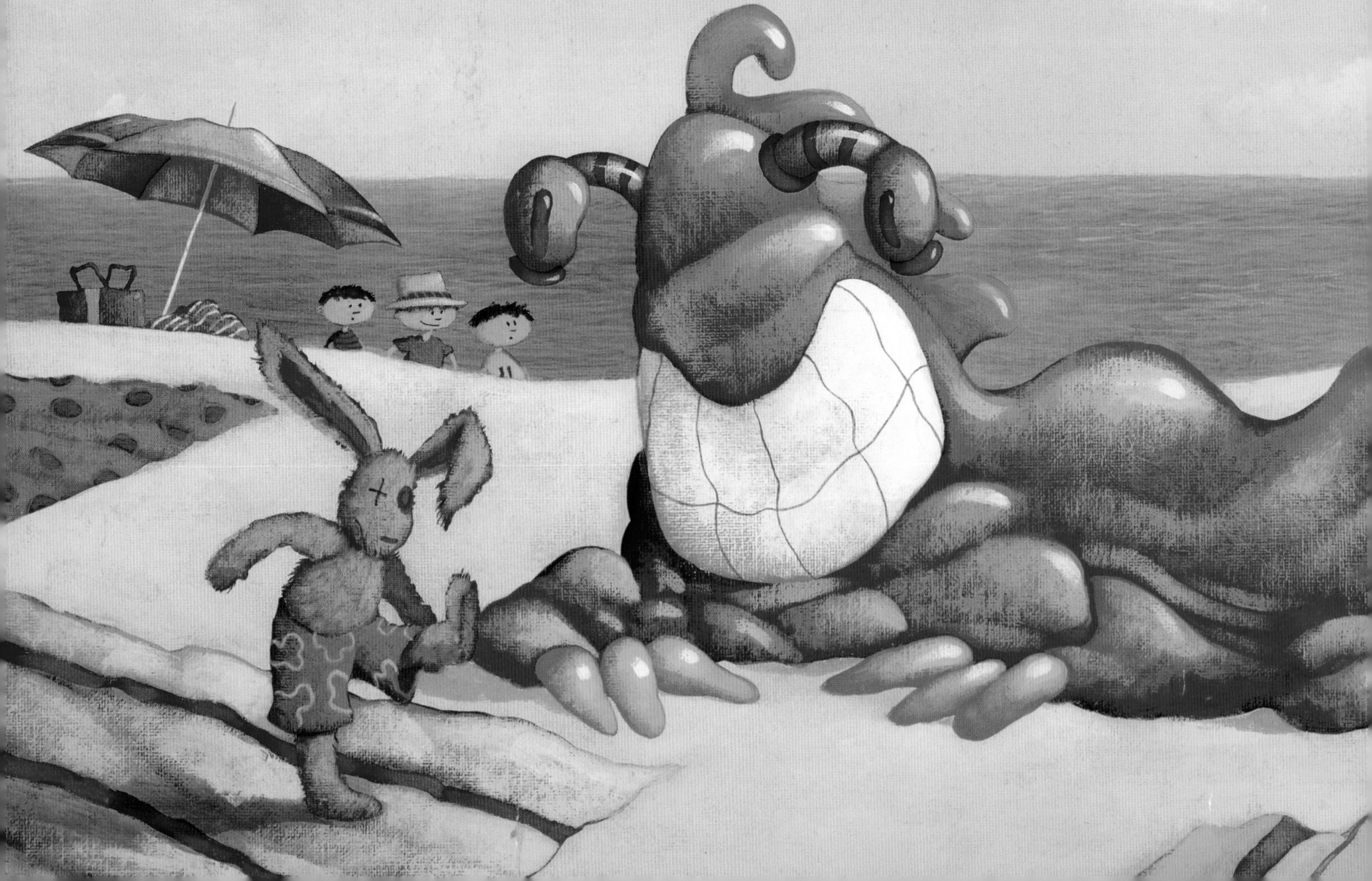

"Enough! Stop! I don't want to explode," said Bob.

Then Taffy and her friends searched for the perfect spot to build the most spectacular sand castle ever.

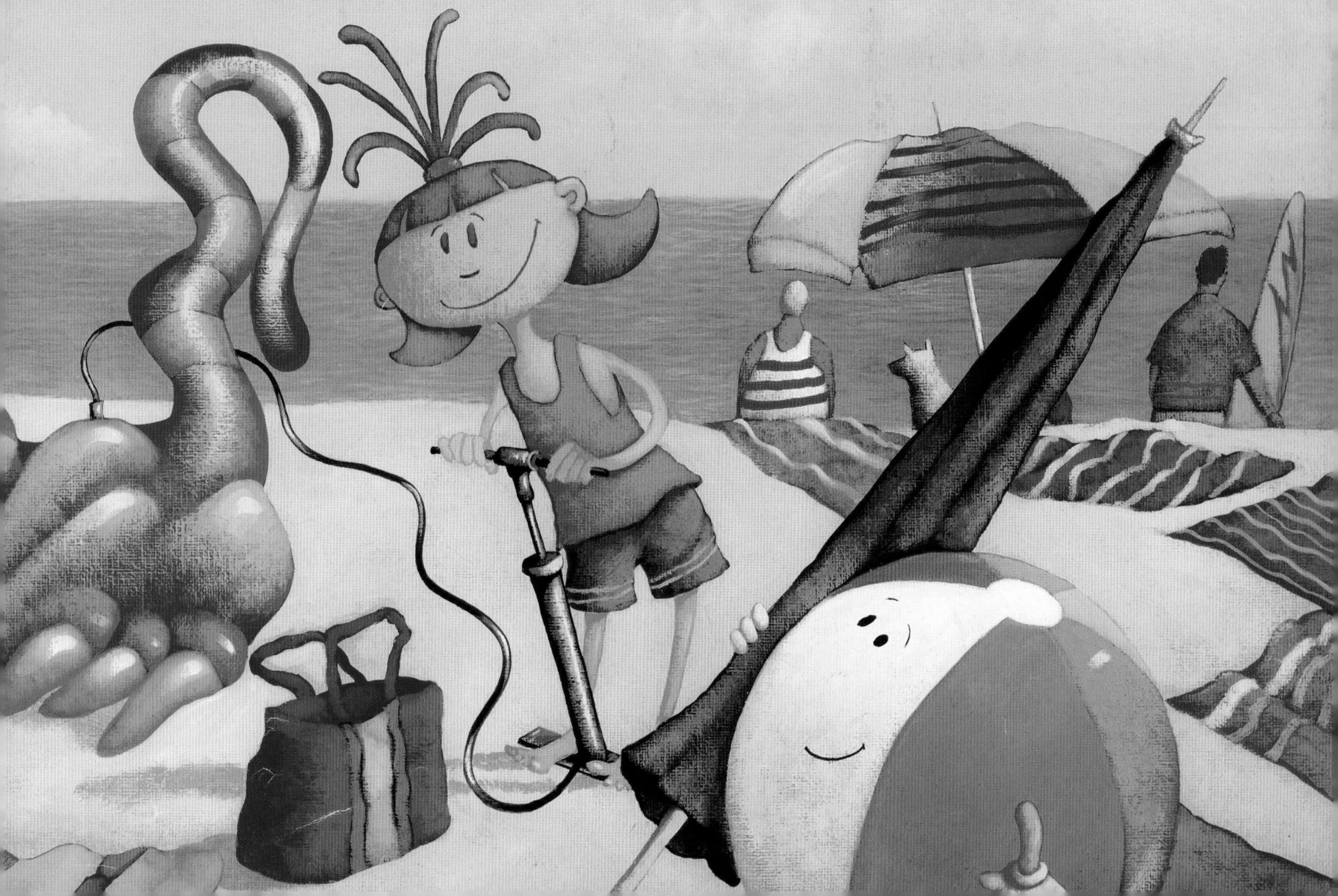

One section was packed with **noisy** families.
Another was covered in **slimy** seaweed.
And a third was **too far** from the water.

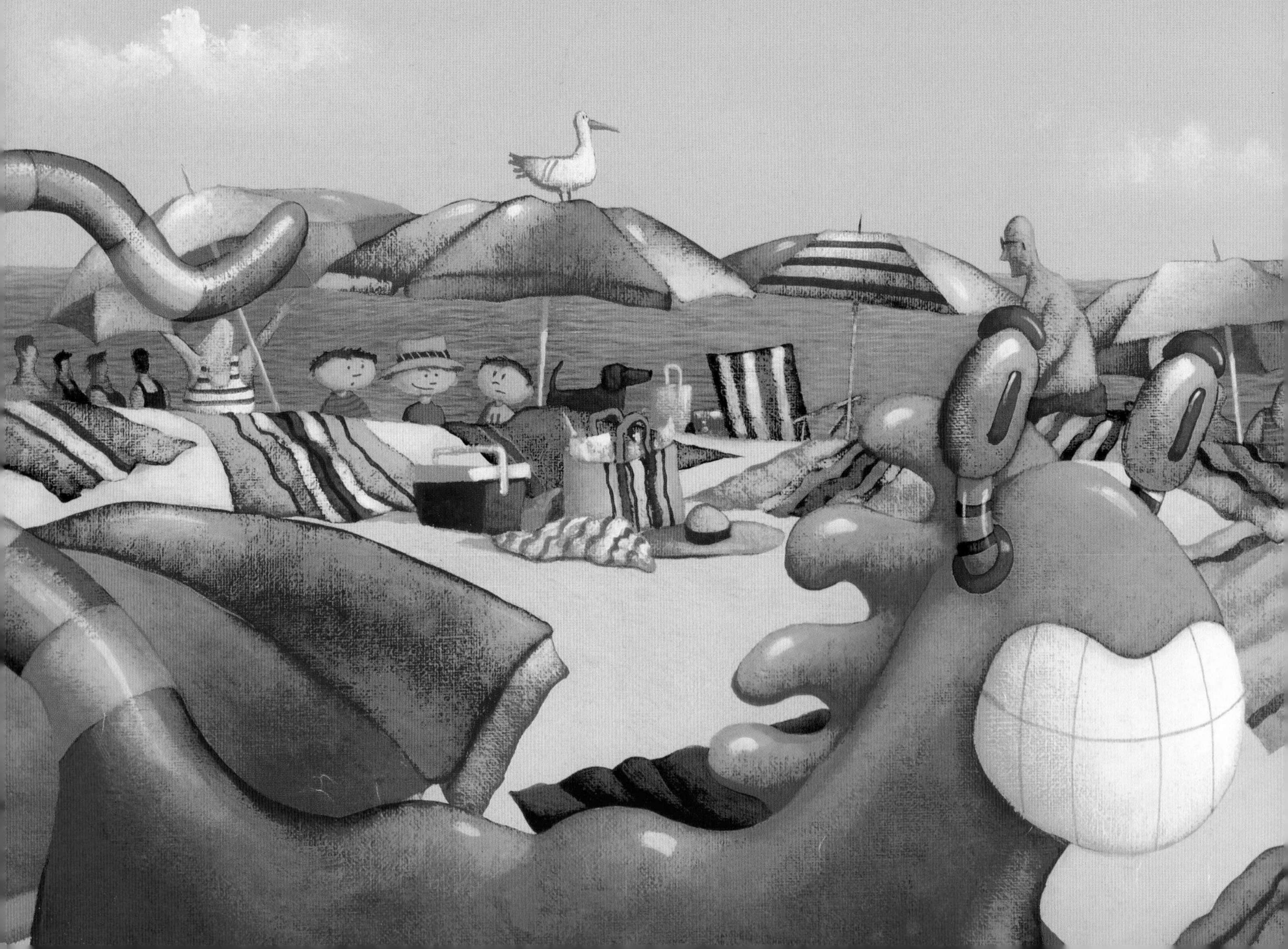

Rigby complained, “We’re not getting anywhere.”
“At least it’s not **windy,**” said Rollo.

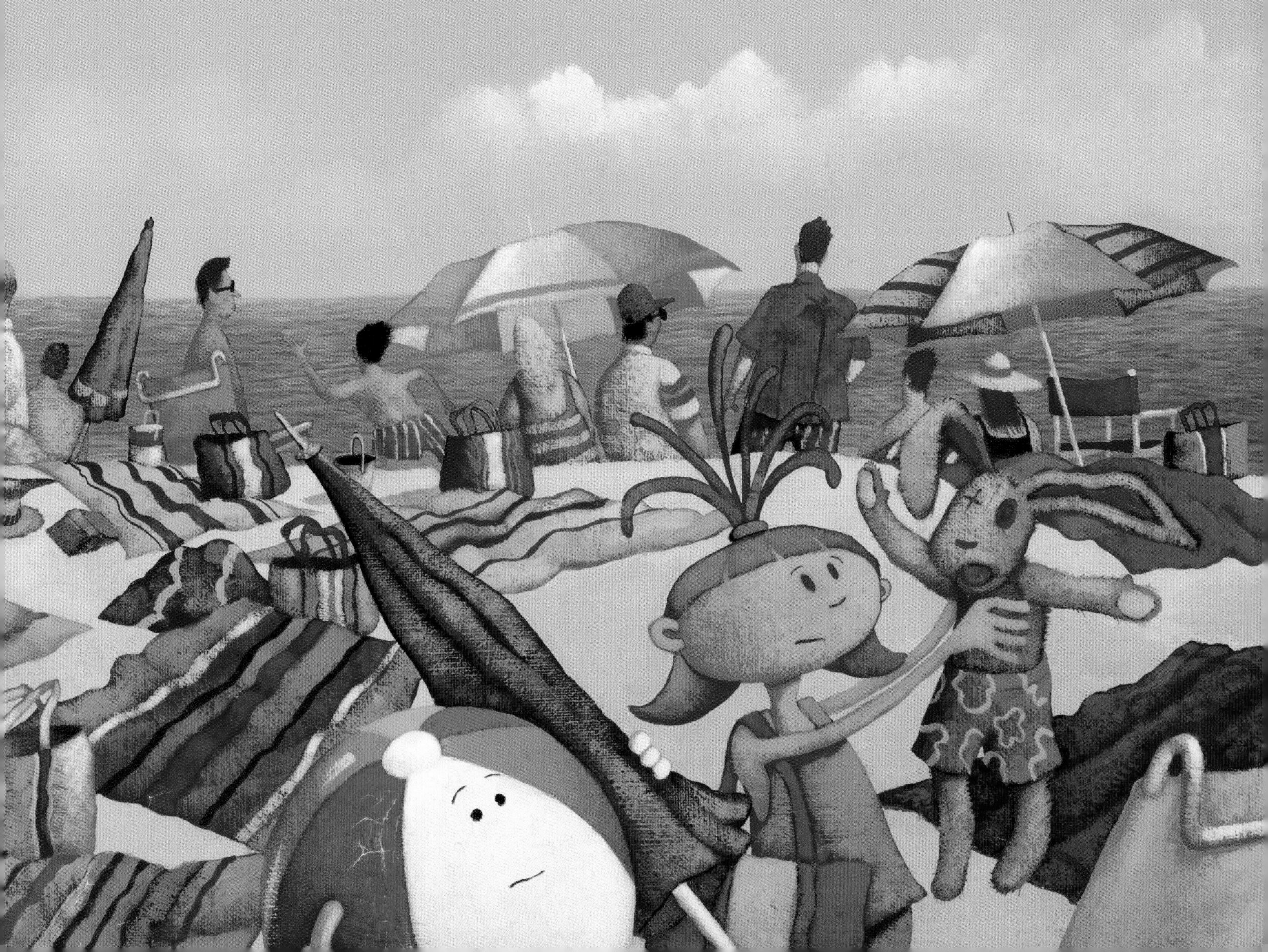

At last Taffy found an empty spot of smooth sand. She picked up a seashell and listened. “I can hear the ocean.”

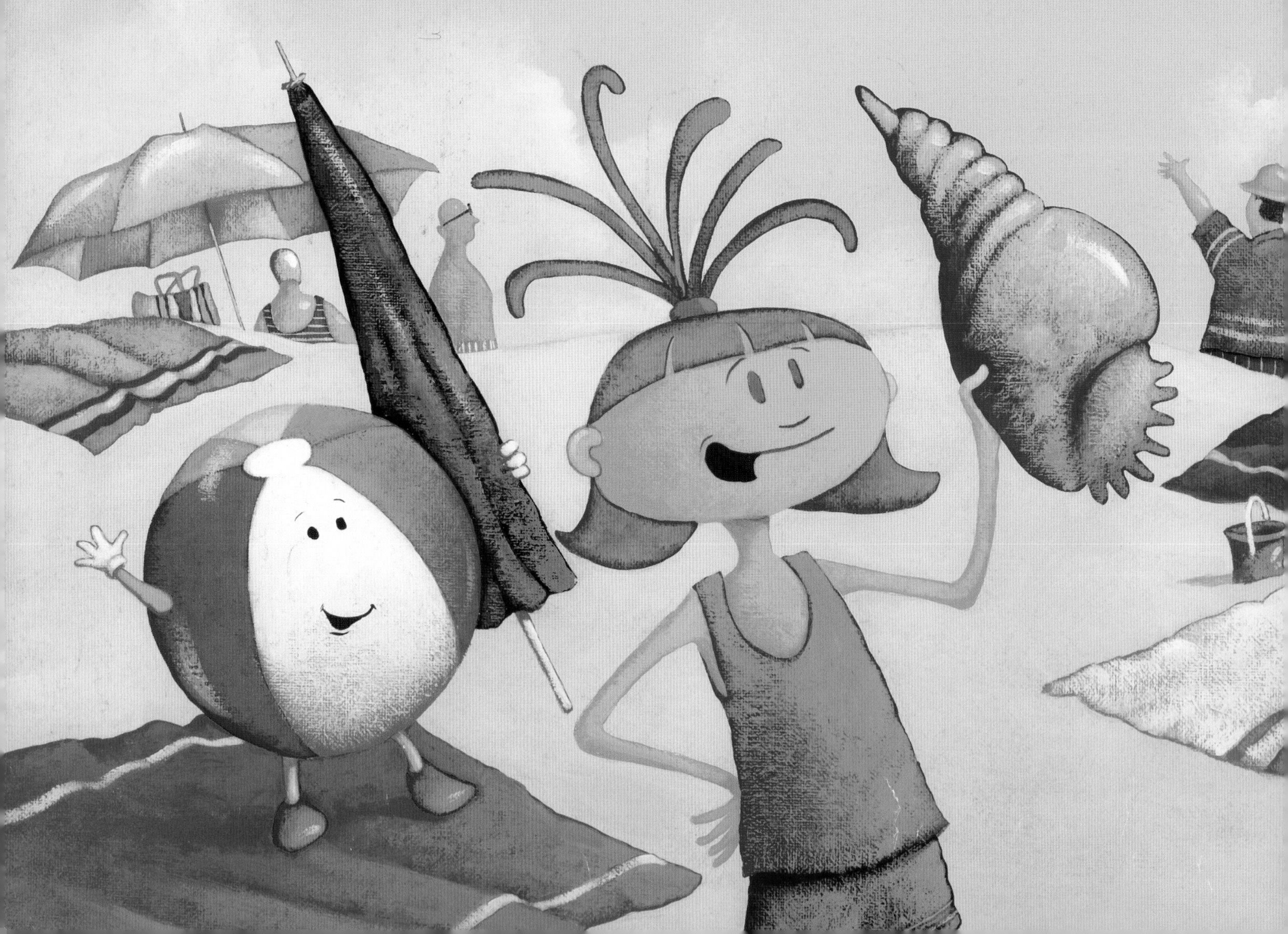

Rollo said, "I'll set up our umbrella."
Rigby sat on his towel. "I'm bored."
"Let the sand-castle building begin," said Taffy.

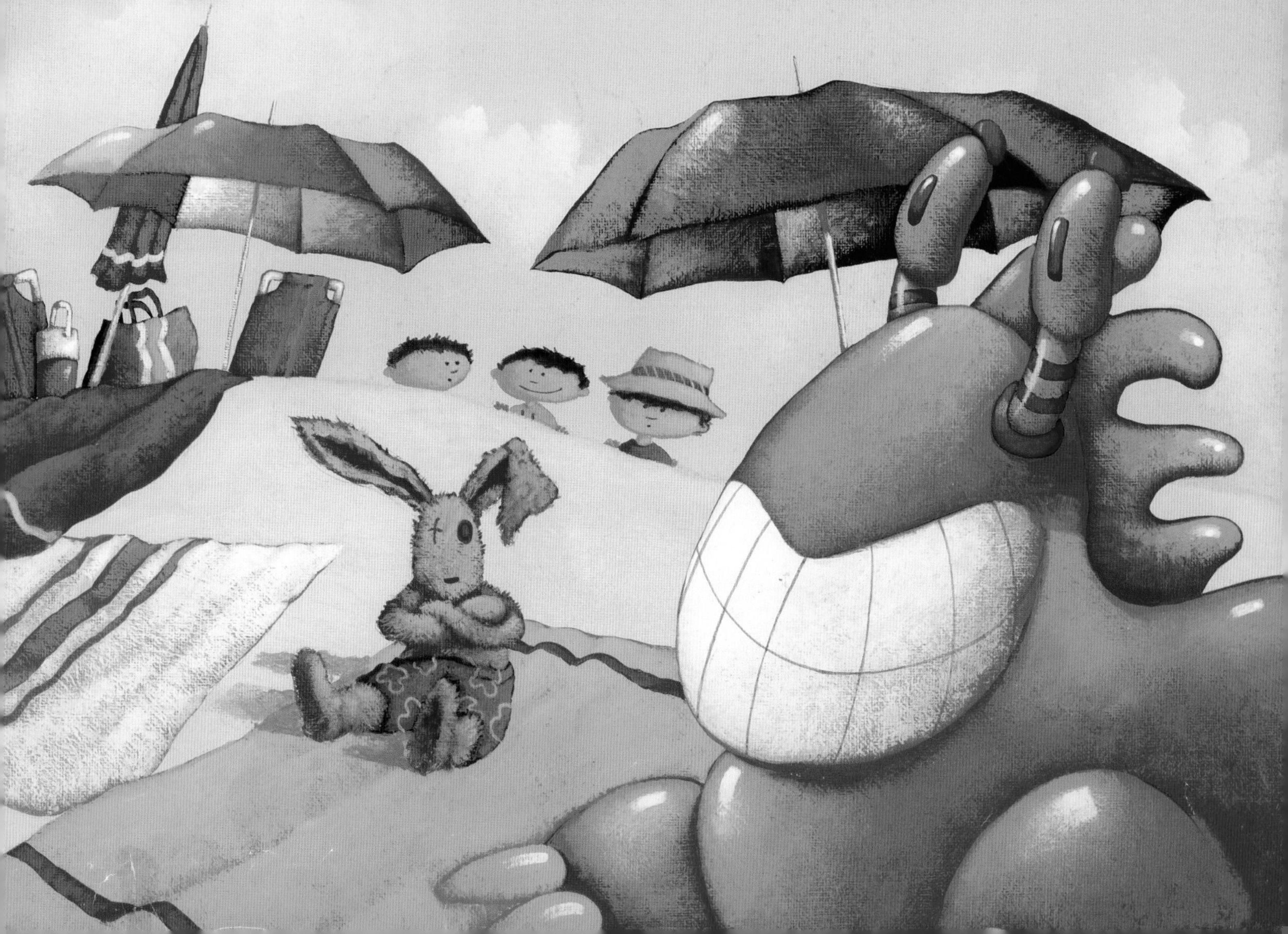

Suddenly, a gust of wind lifted Rollo and the beach umbrella high into the air.

"Help, Taffy, help!"

"Hang on, Rollo," Taffy shouted.

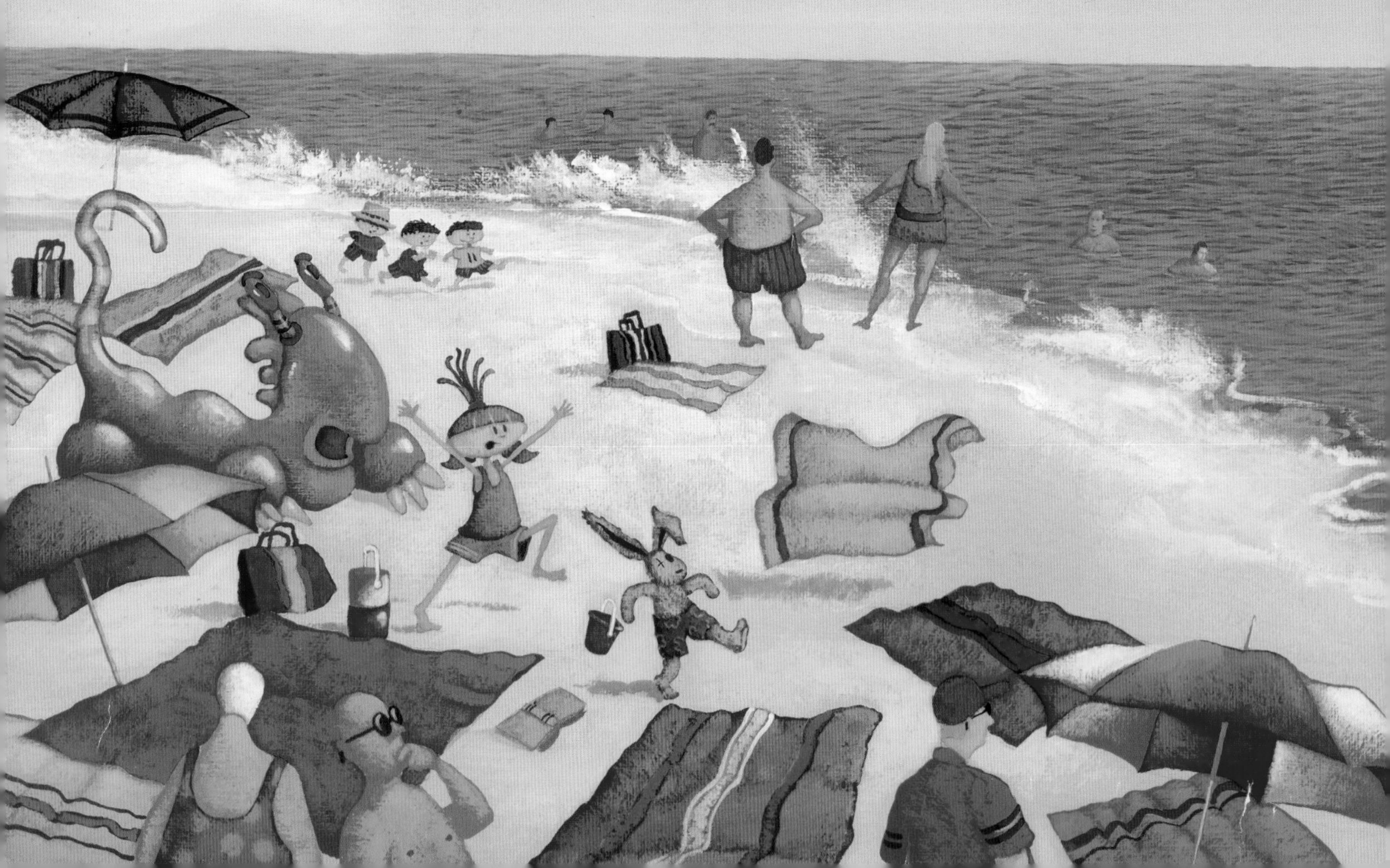

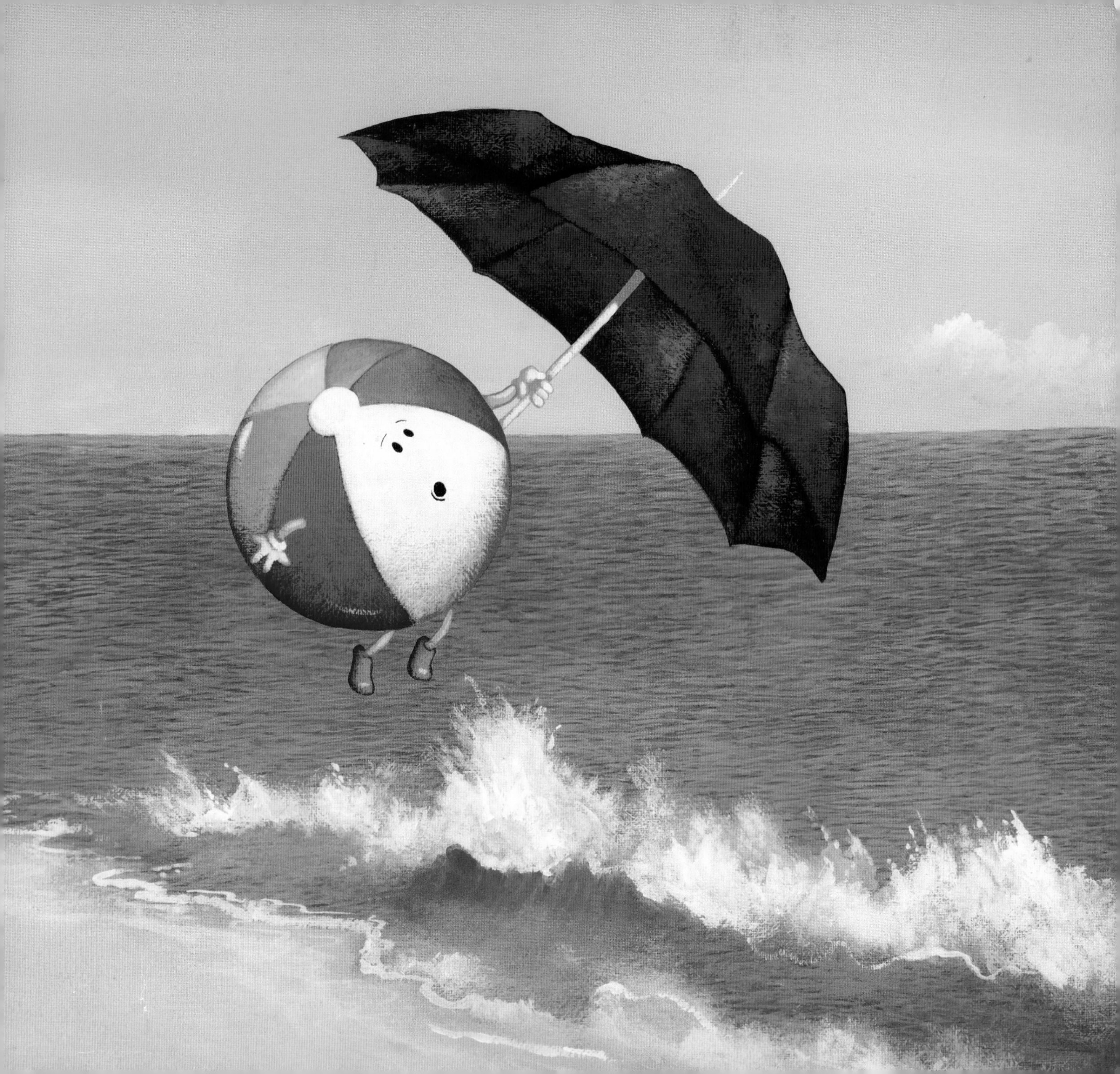

Taffy jumped on Bob's back. "Hurry."

"Don't forget *me*!" said a very grumpy Rigby.

"We're coming," yelled Bob.

They raced down the beach, picking up Chris . . . and Edna . . . and Mr. Footer.

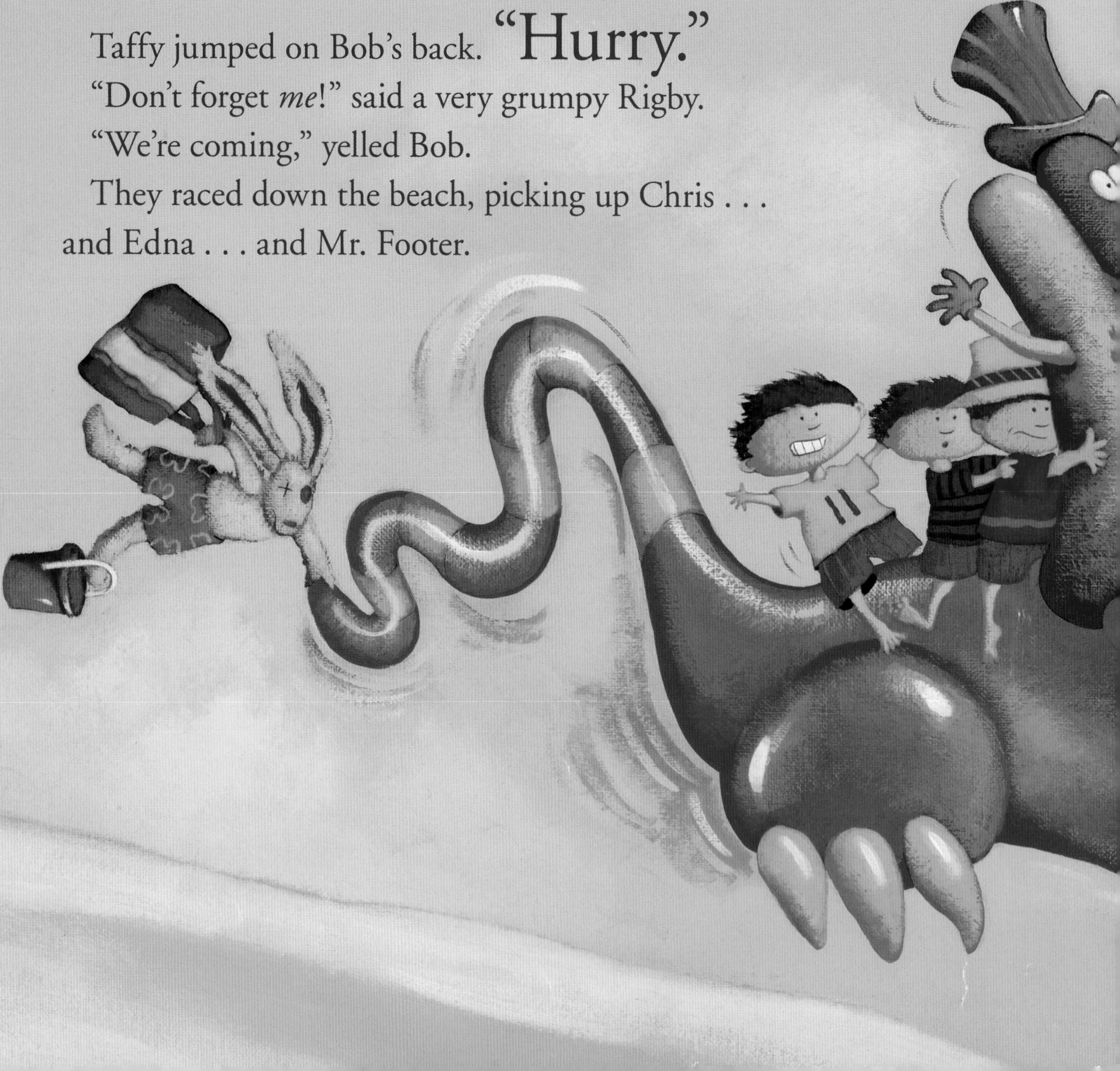

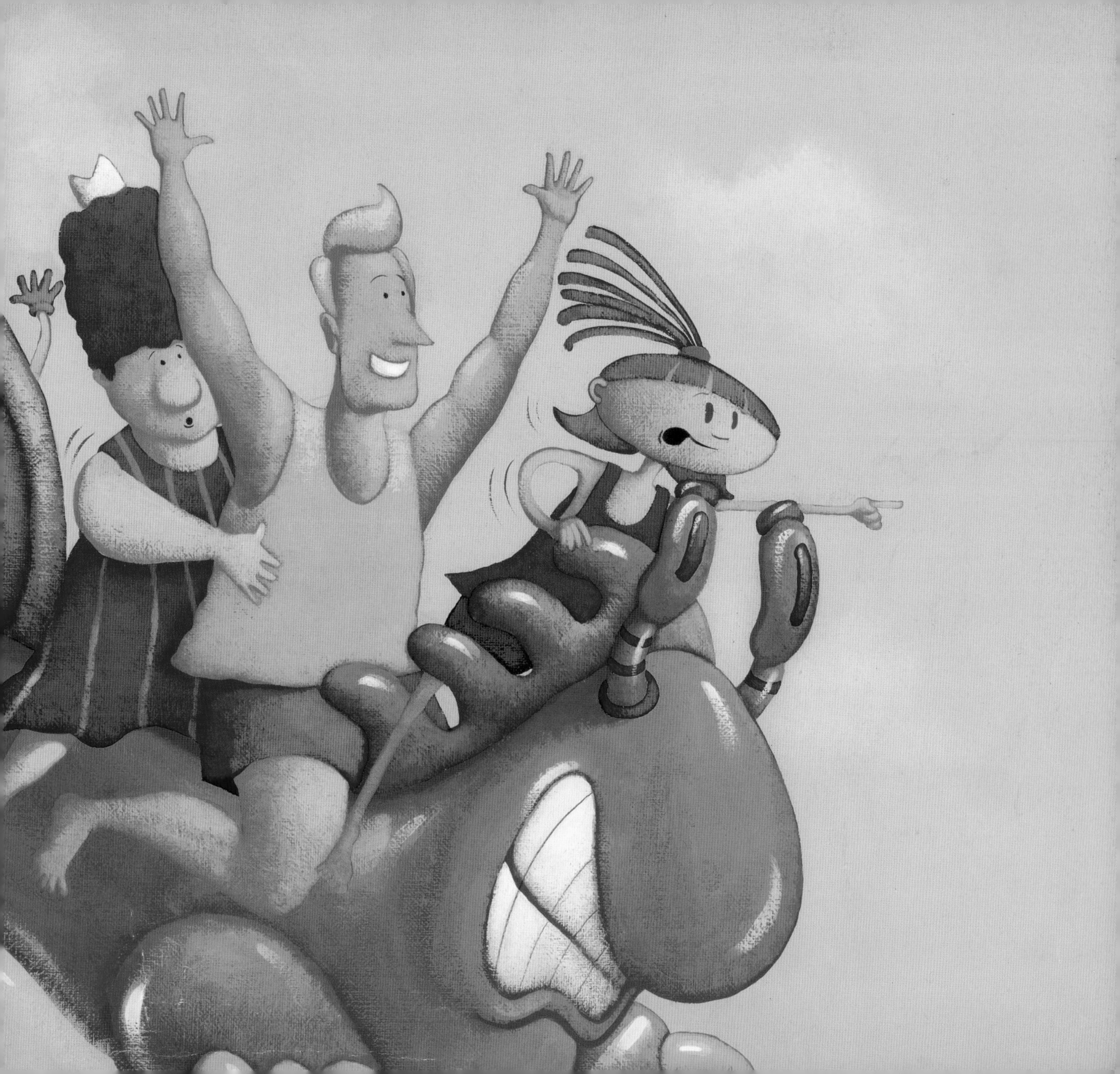

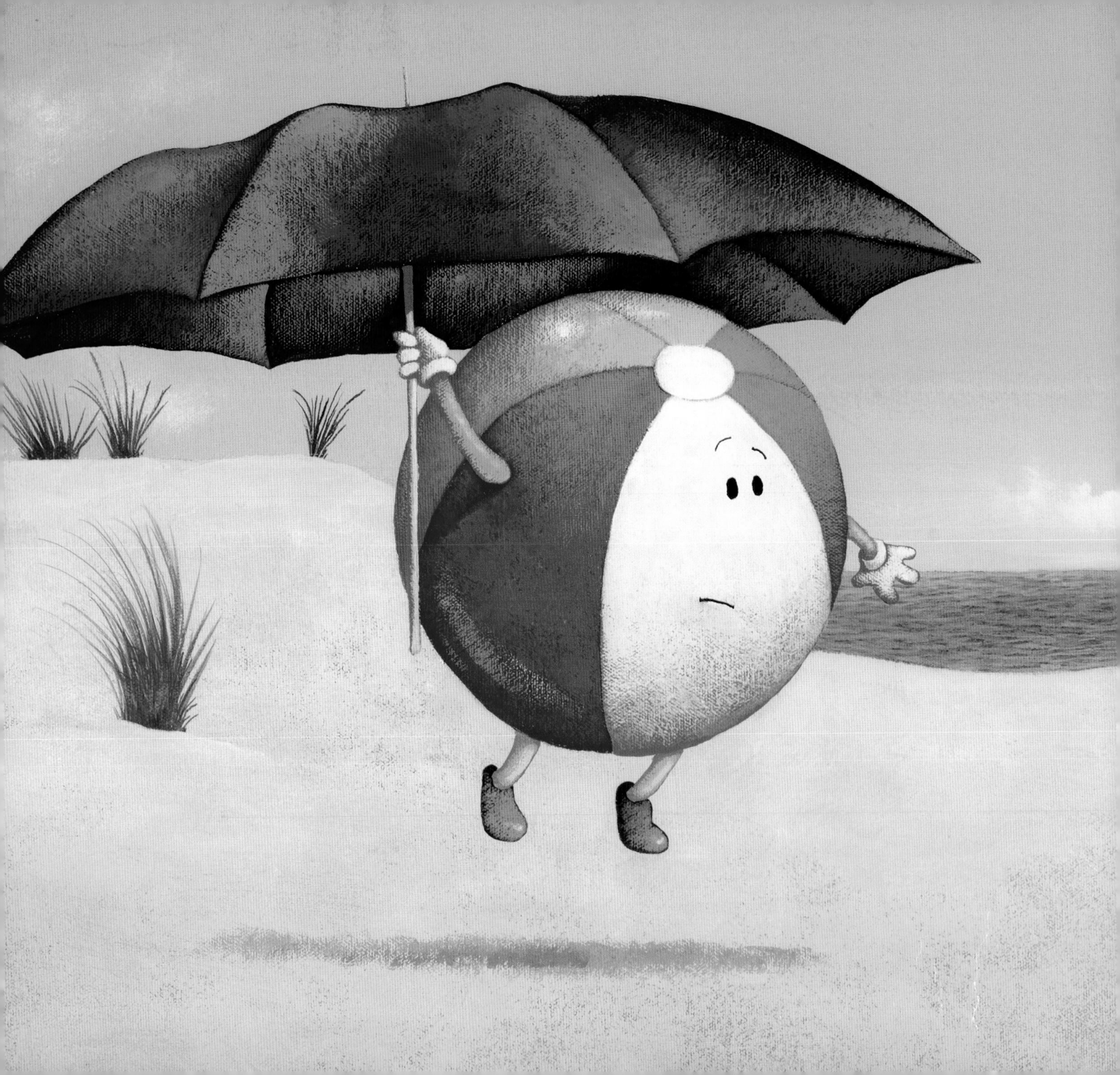

Way, way, waaaaaay down the beach, a nervous Rollo landed on the soft sand with a thump.

"I'm lost," he said to a seagull. Then he added, "That's a sharp beak. I need to be careful of pointy objects."

The seagull said nothing.

Rollo felt another breeze. "Oh, no, it's getting **windy** again."

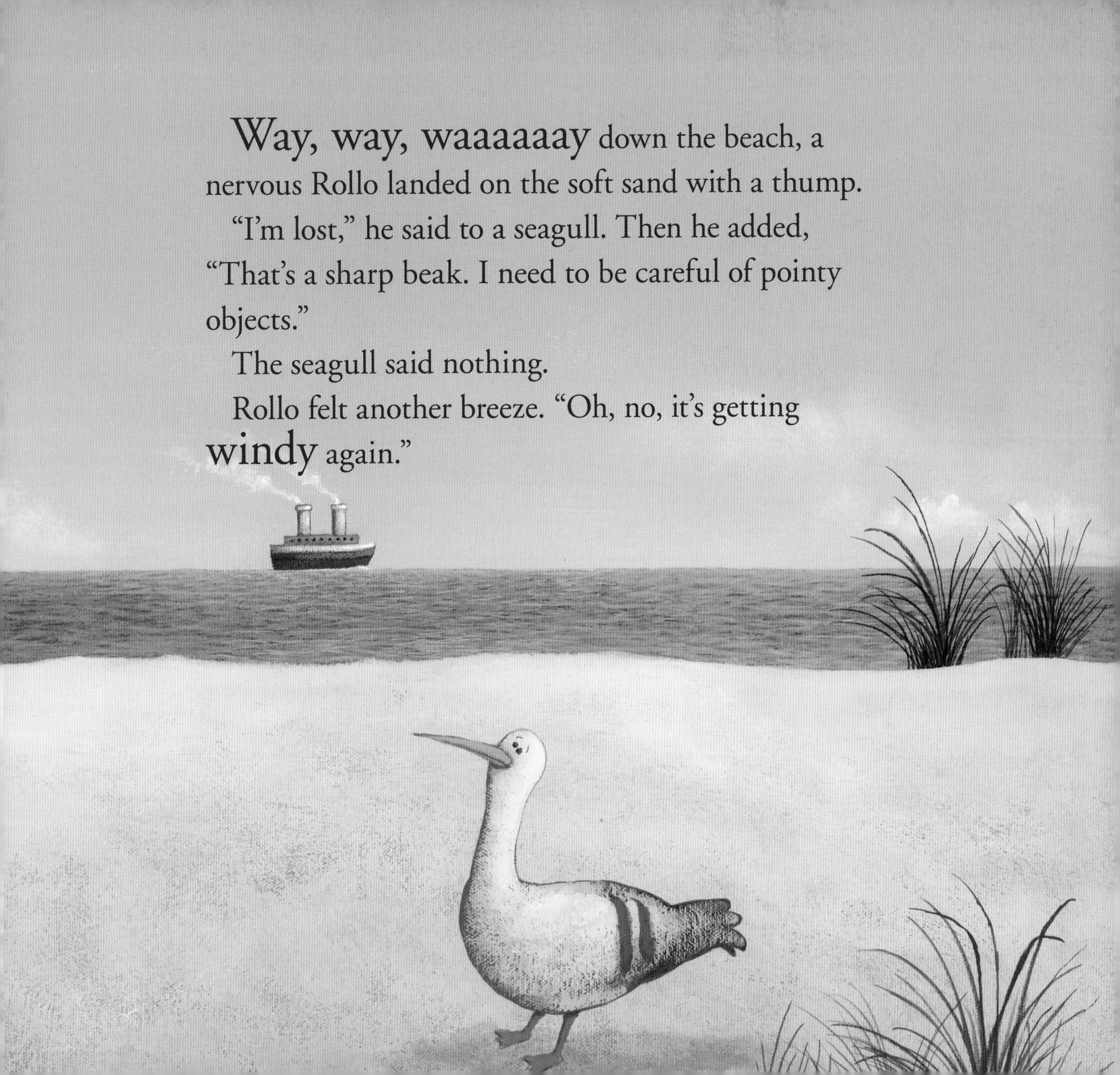

Without a word, the seagull flew off.
"Silly bird."

Rollo worried he would never see his friends again.

Just then the seagull returned, carrying a beach towel. He dropped the towel on Rollo right as the wind picked up.

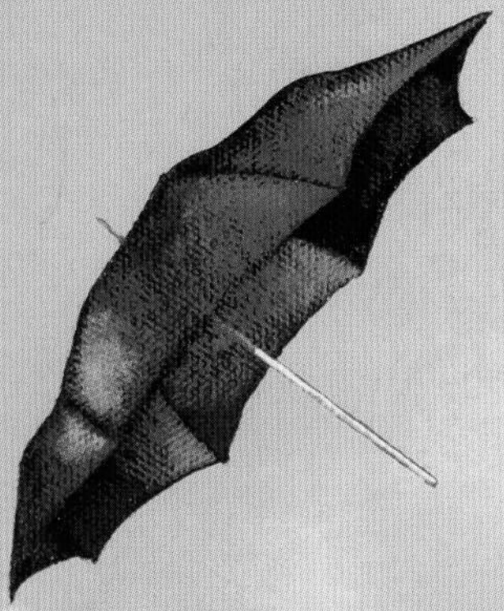

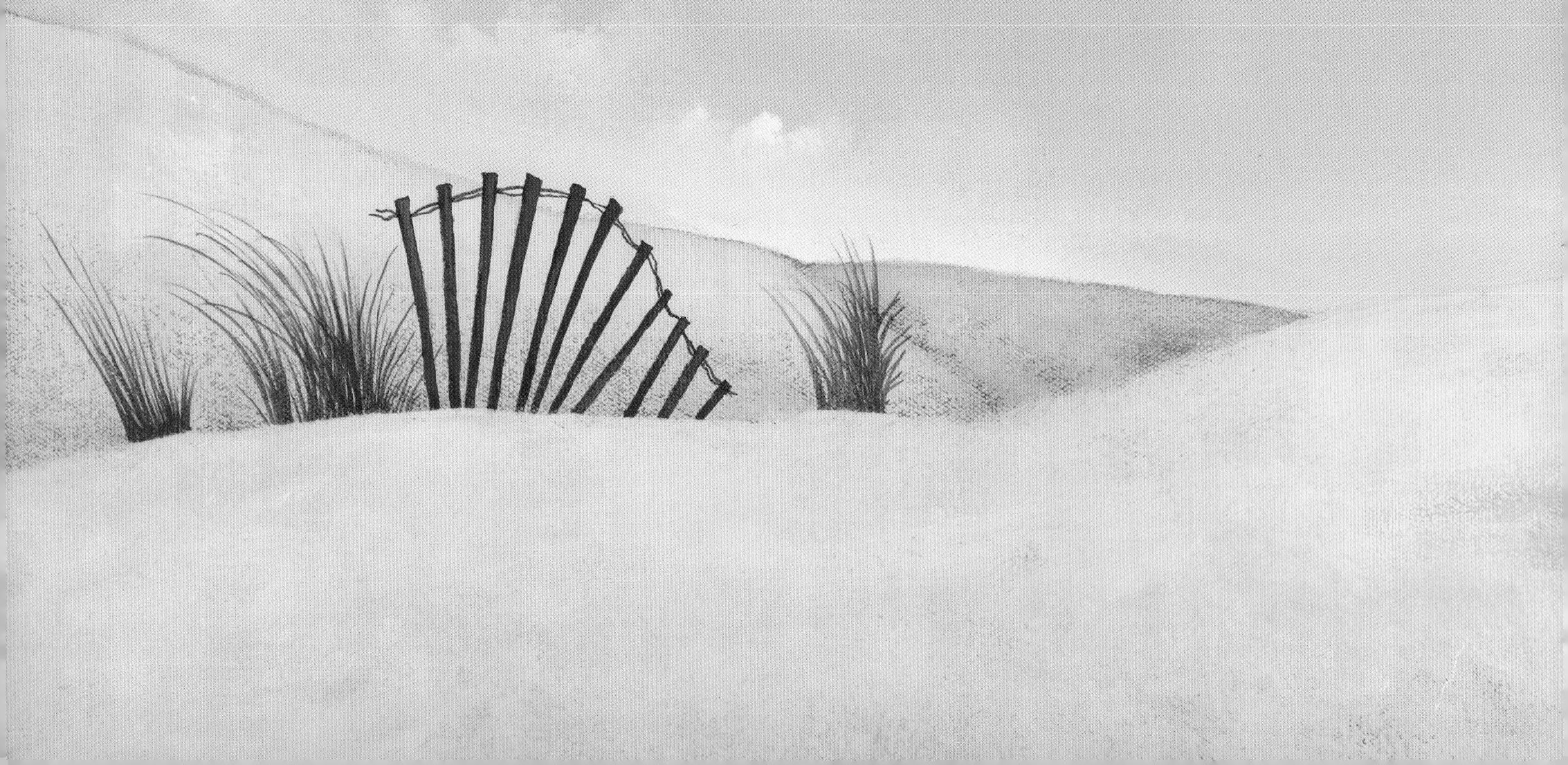

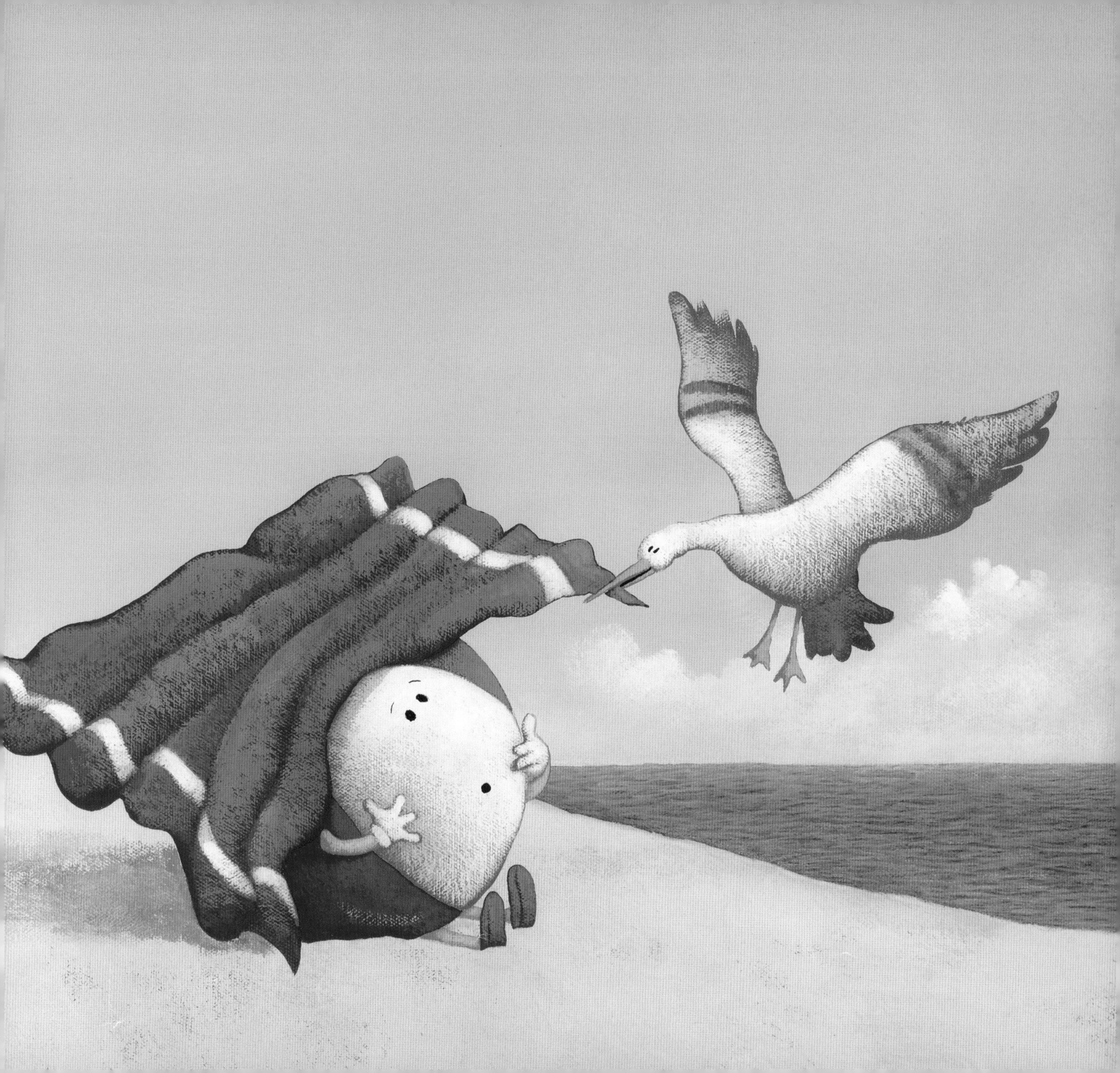

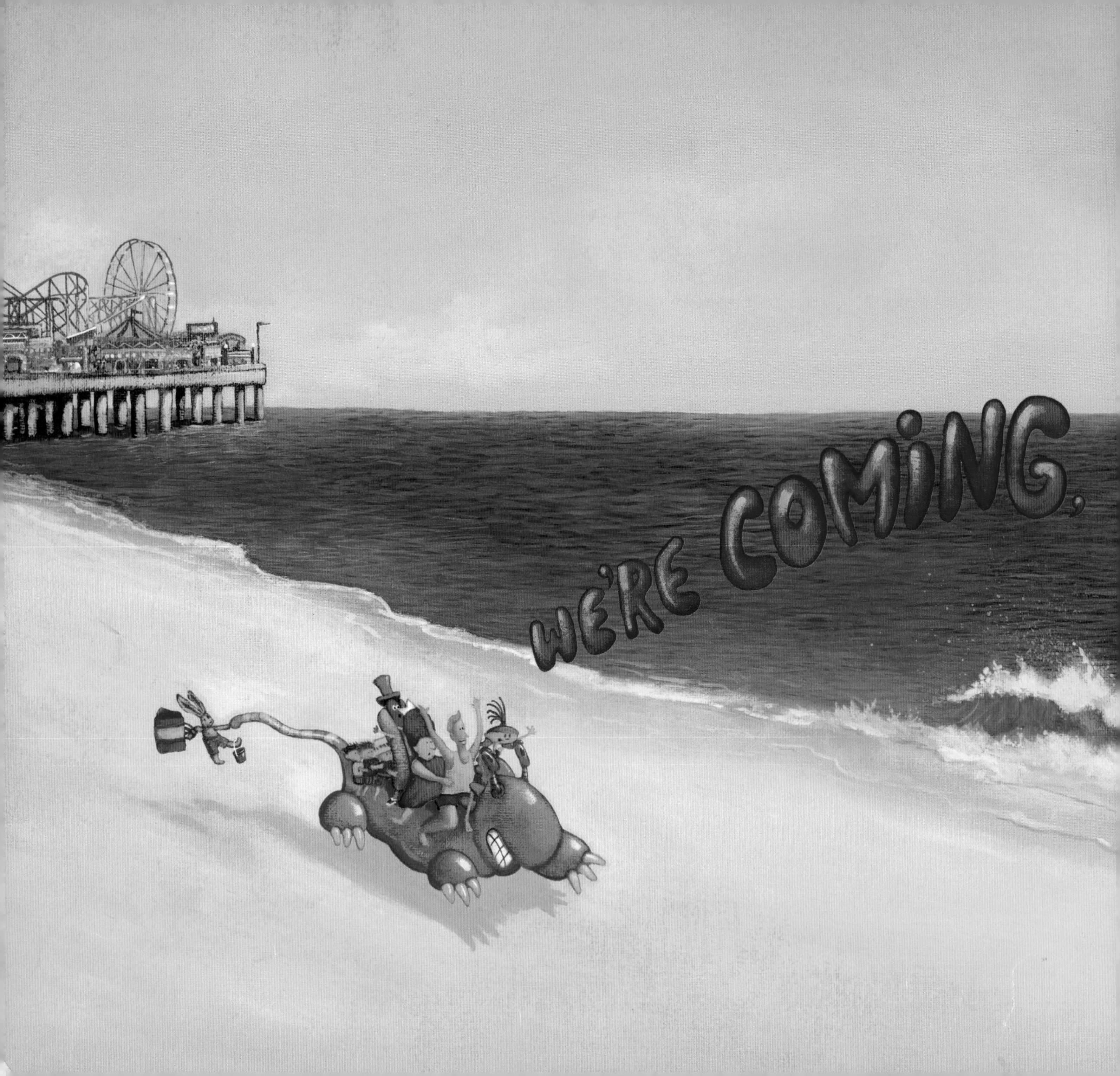
WE'RE COMING,

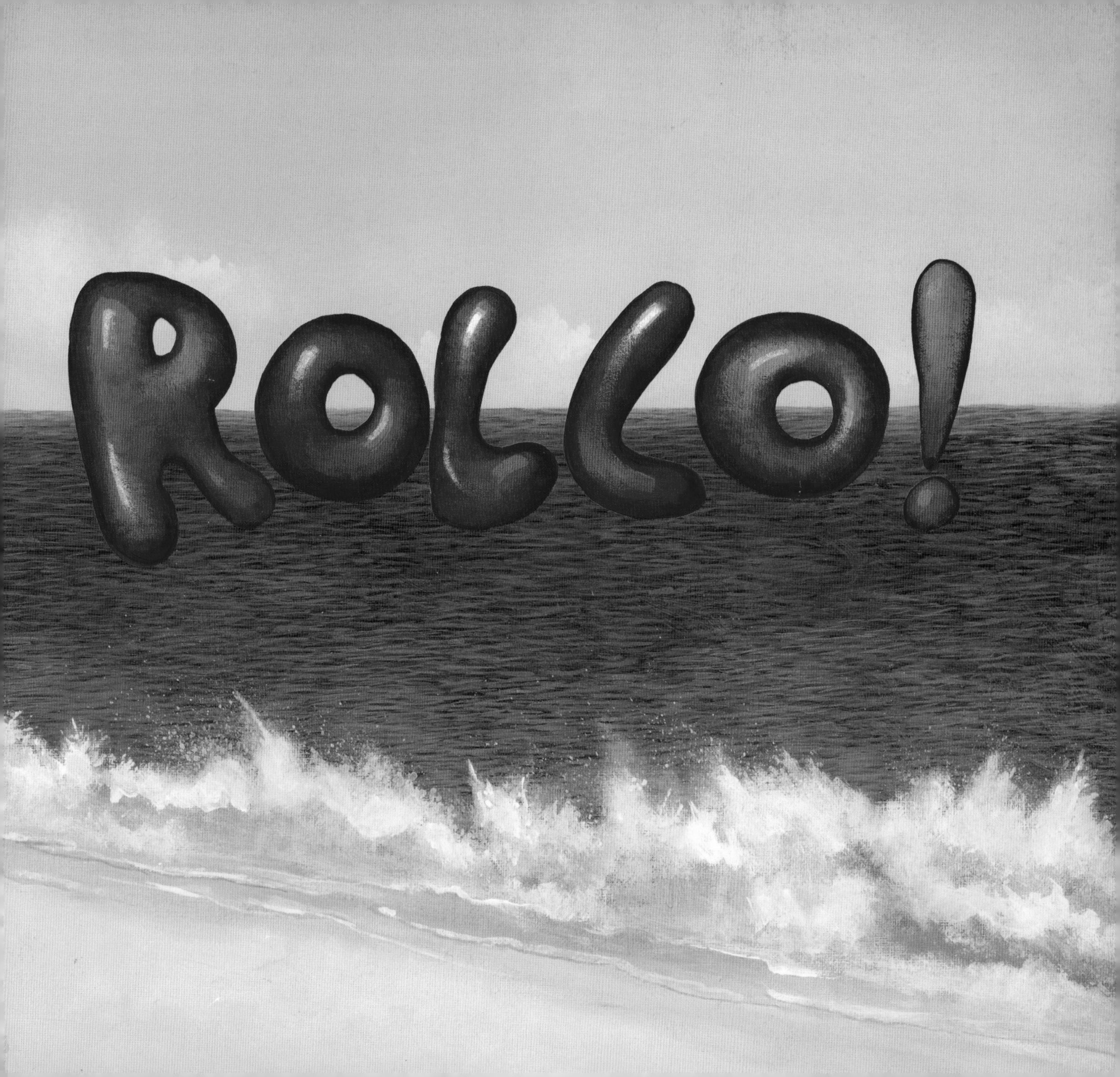
ROLLO!

Bob galumphed into view.

Taffy shouted, “There he is, look!”

“This is my new buddy,” said a happy Rollo. “He doesn’t say much, but he saved me from blowing away.”

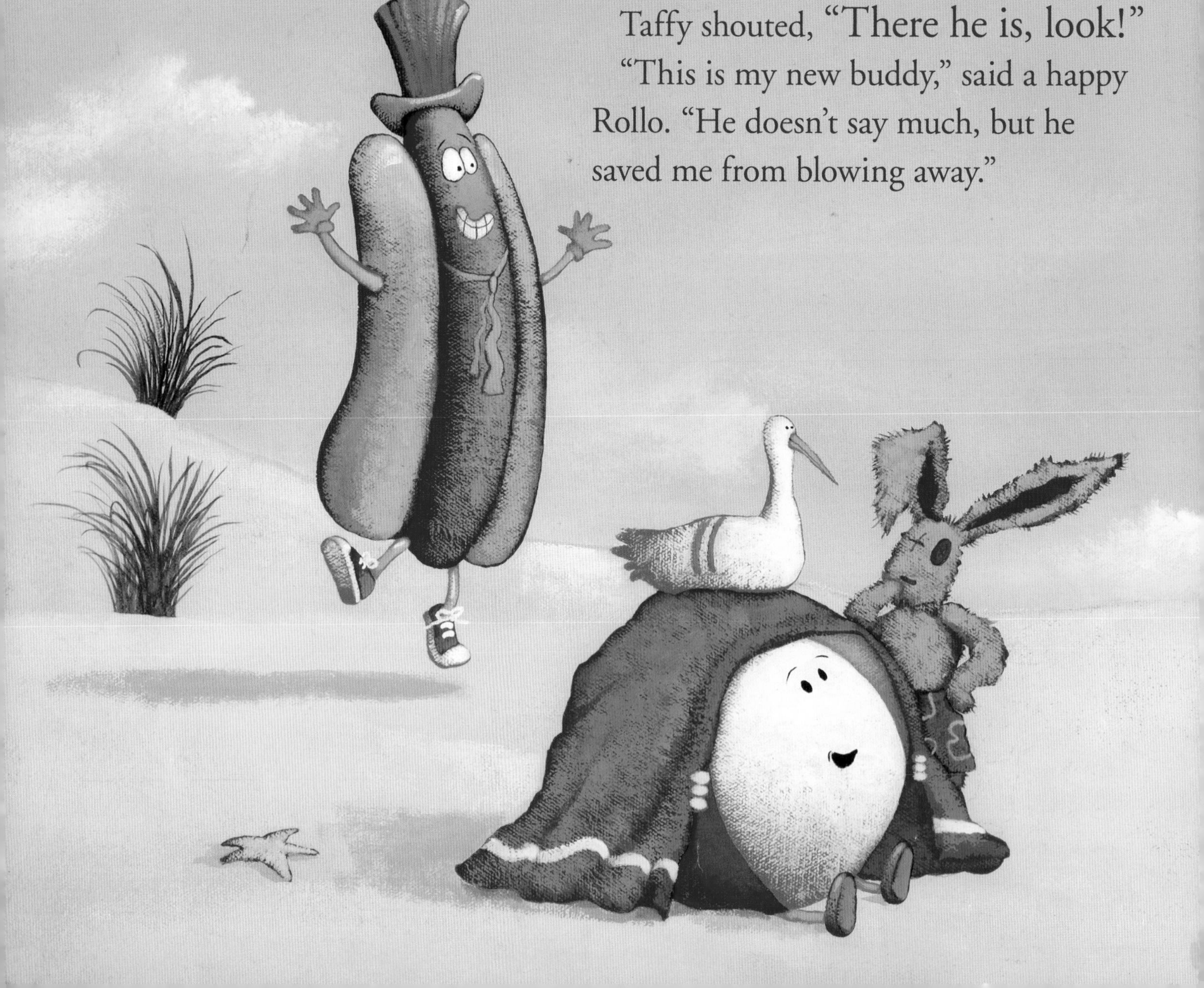

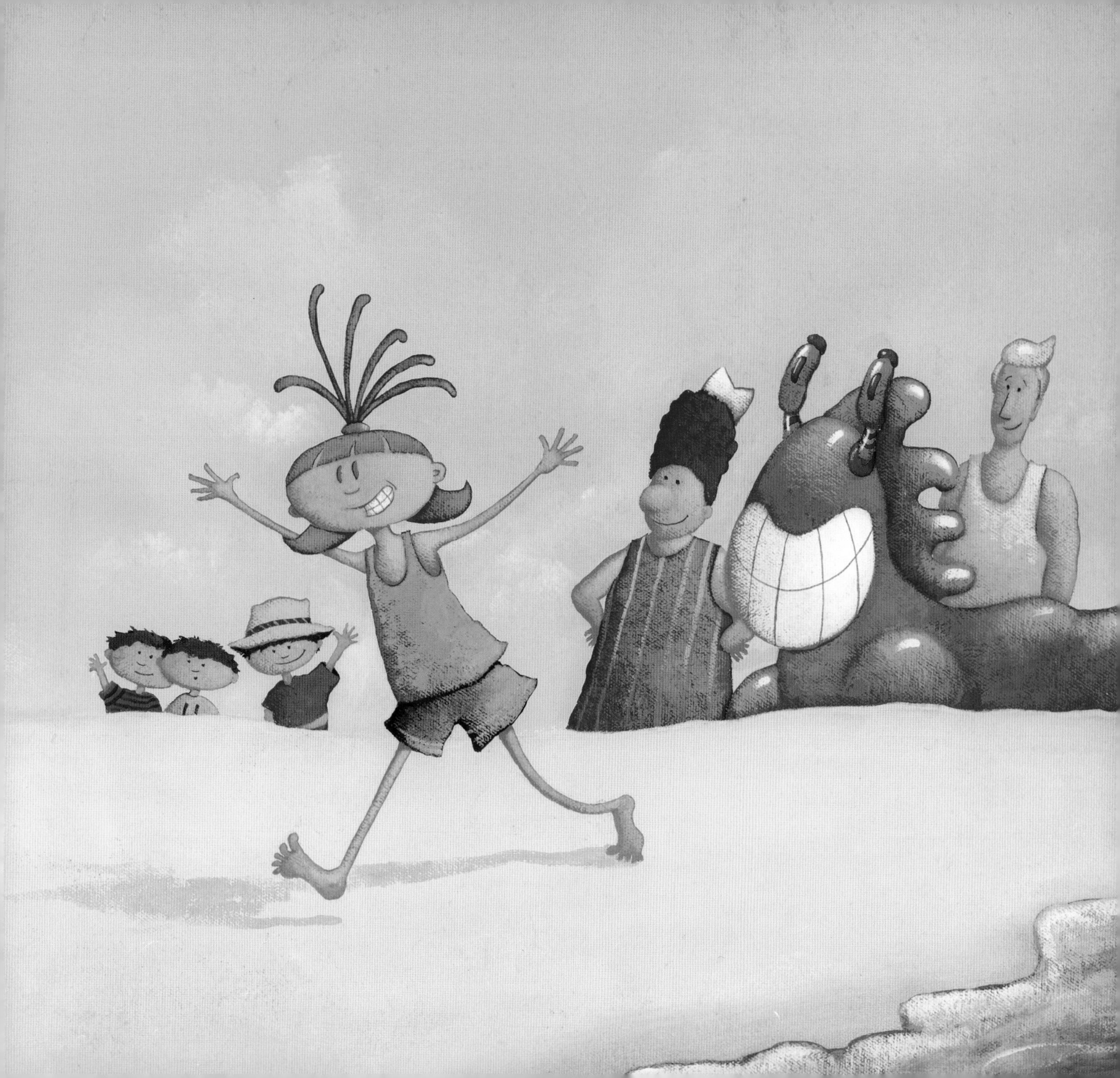

Rigby shook out his furry feet. "We're never going to build anything."

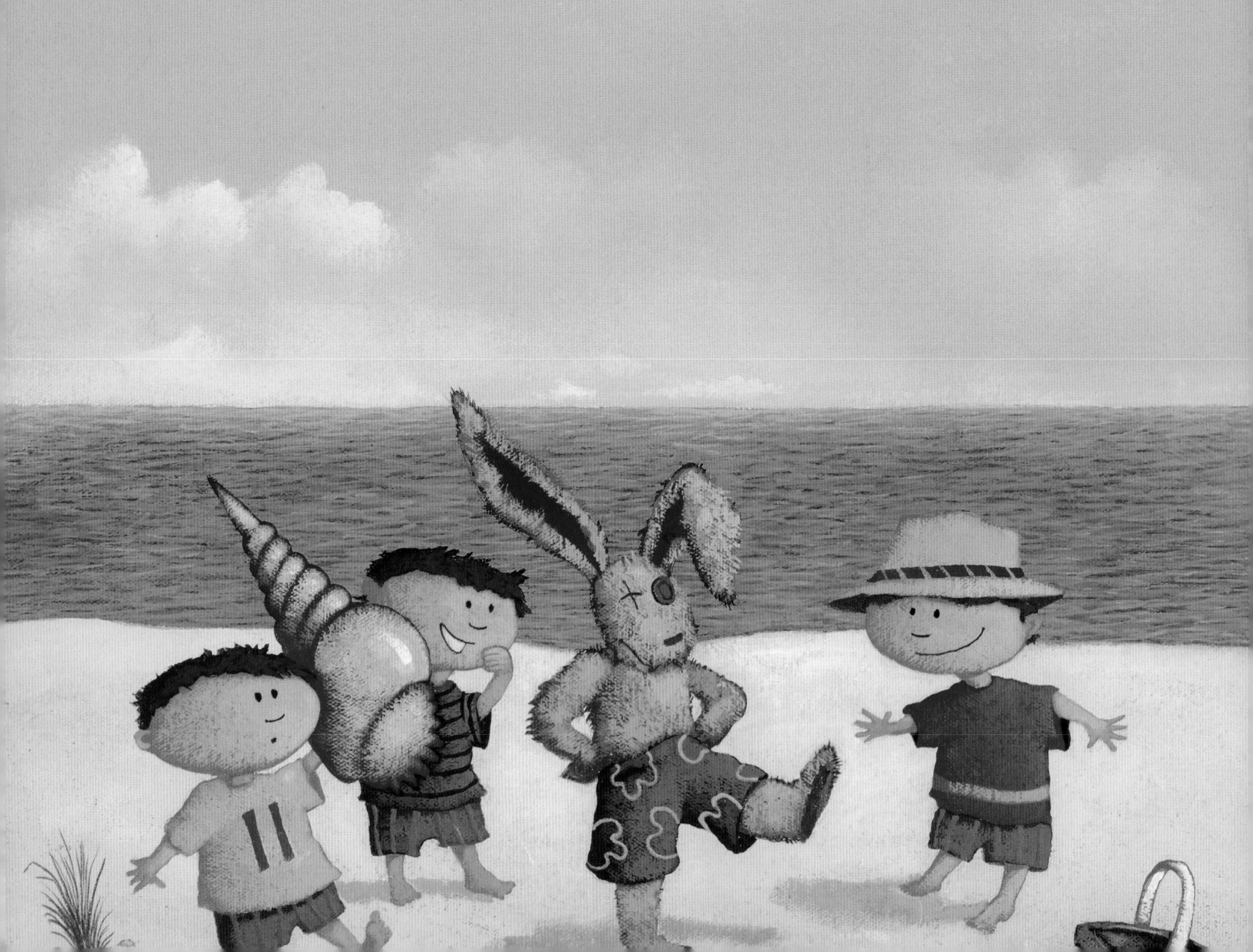

Taffy looked around and said, “Rollo, I think you found the perfect spot for a spectacular sand castle.”

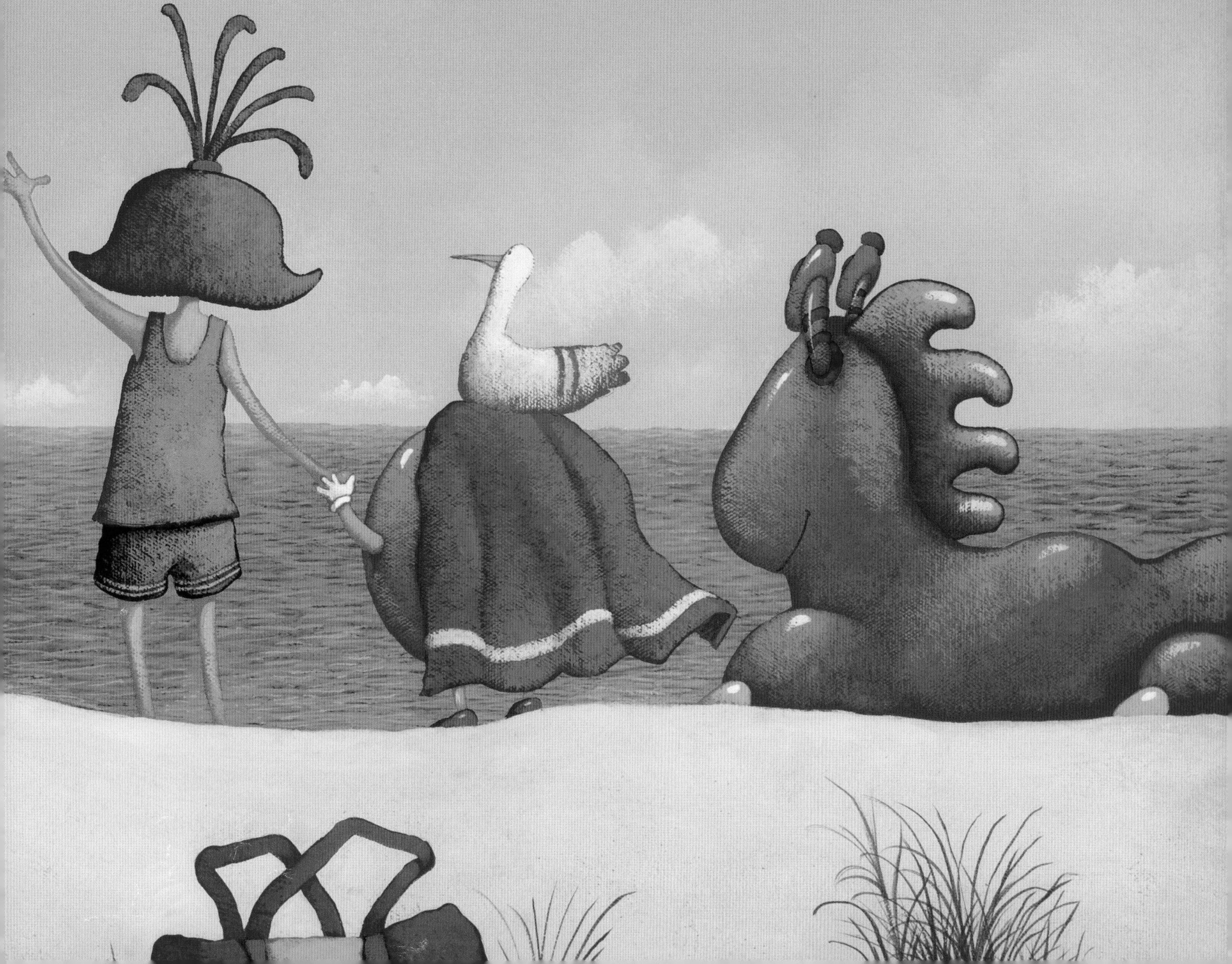

They **dug** and **dug** and **shaped** and **scraped** in the yummy summer sun. Rigby helped, but he stood on a towel so his furry feet did not touch the sand.

Edna served her coldest, sweetest lemon-ice.

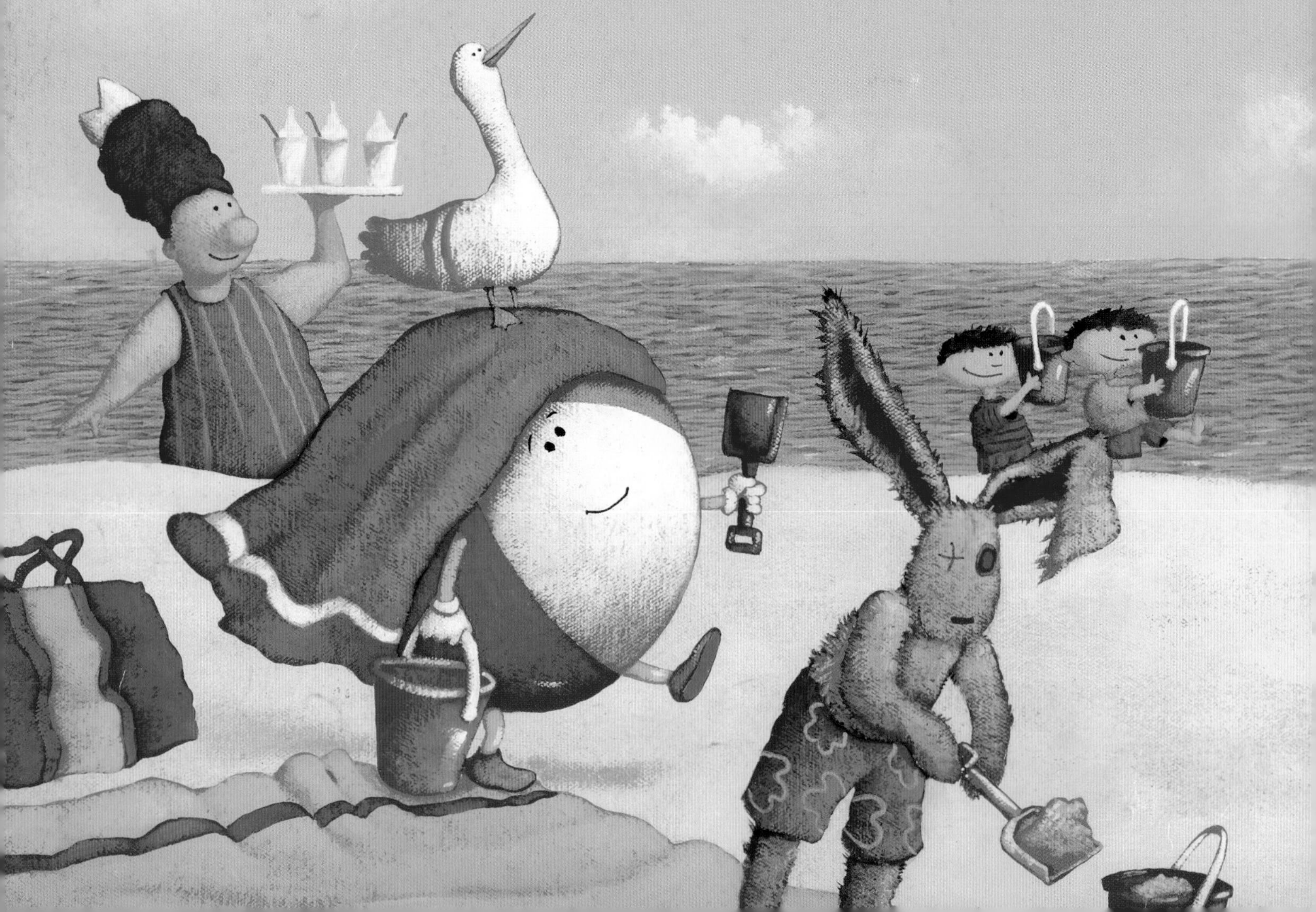

Finally it was finished.

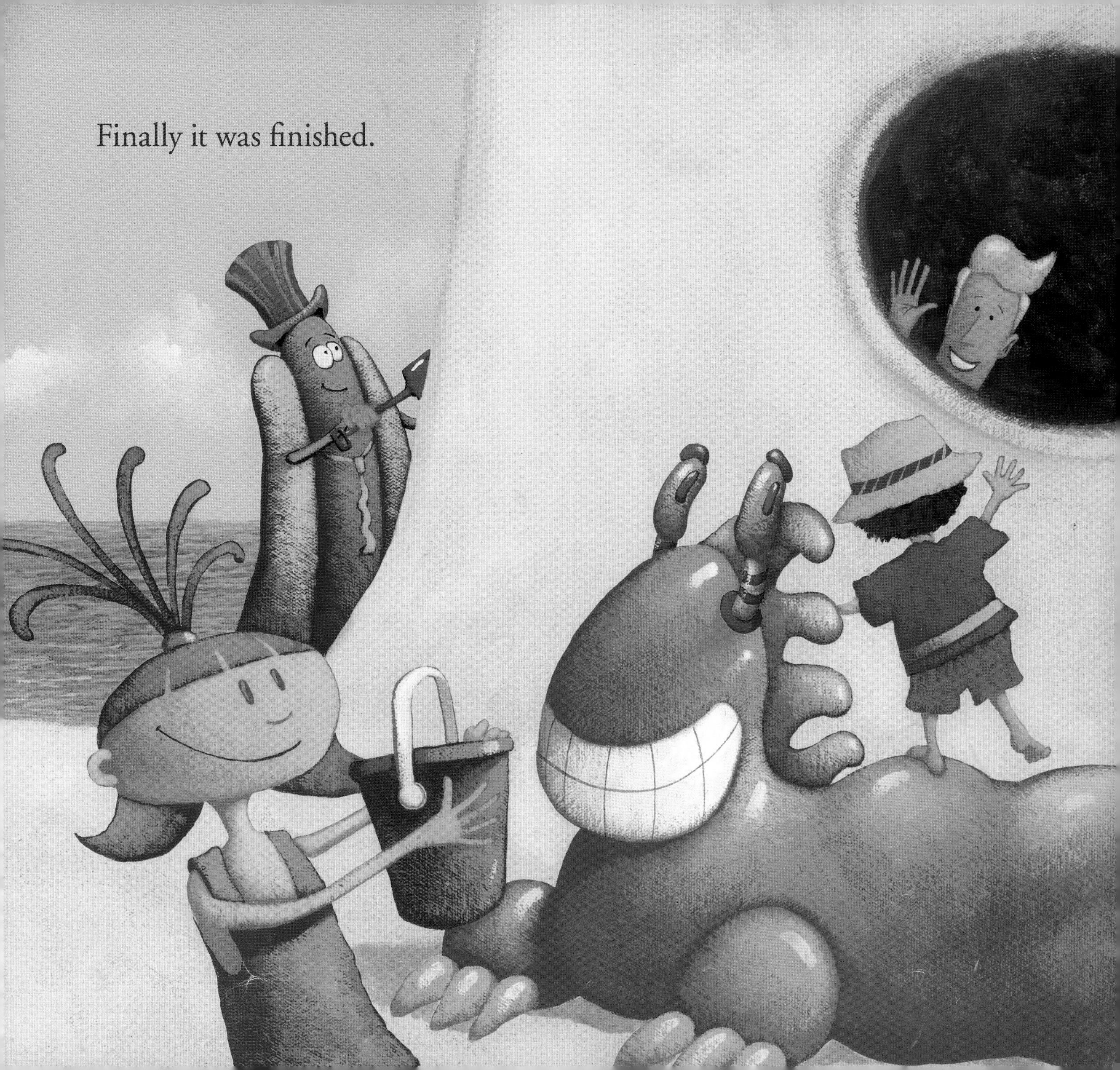

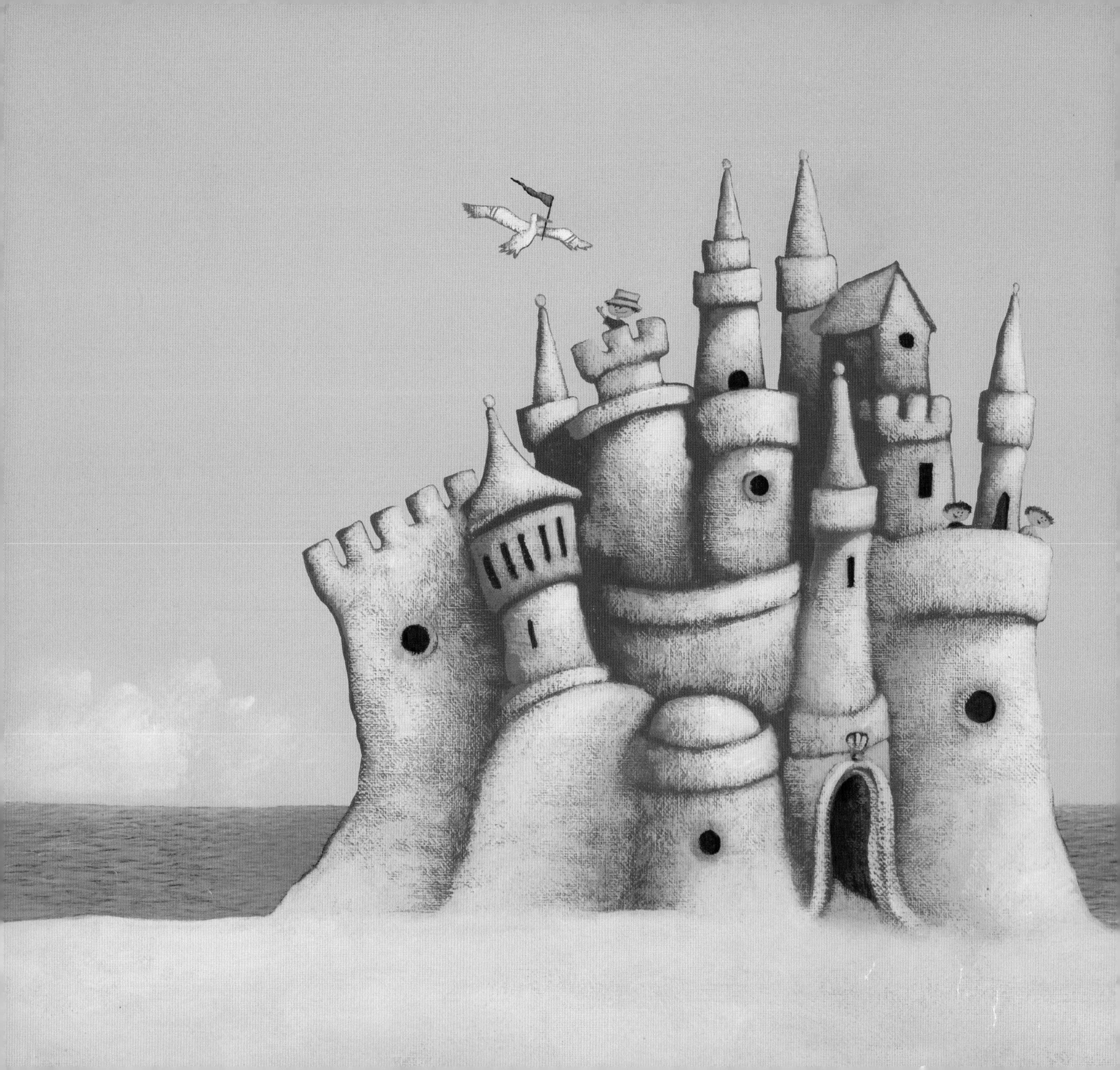

The seagull crowned the highest tower with
a flag made from Mr. Footer's handkerchief.
Everyone cheered.

“Wasn’t that fun, Rigby? Even if you did get some sand in your furry feet?”

Rigby looked up at the spectacular sand castle. At last he smiled and said, “I guess we could come back tomorrow.”

Taffy laughed and gave him a big hug.

Rollo bounced up and down. “What are we going to do?”

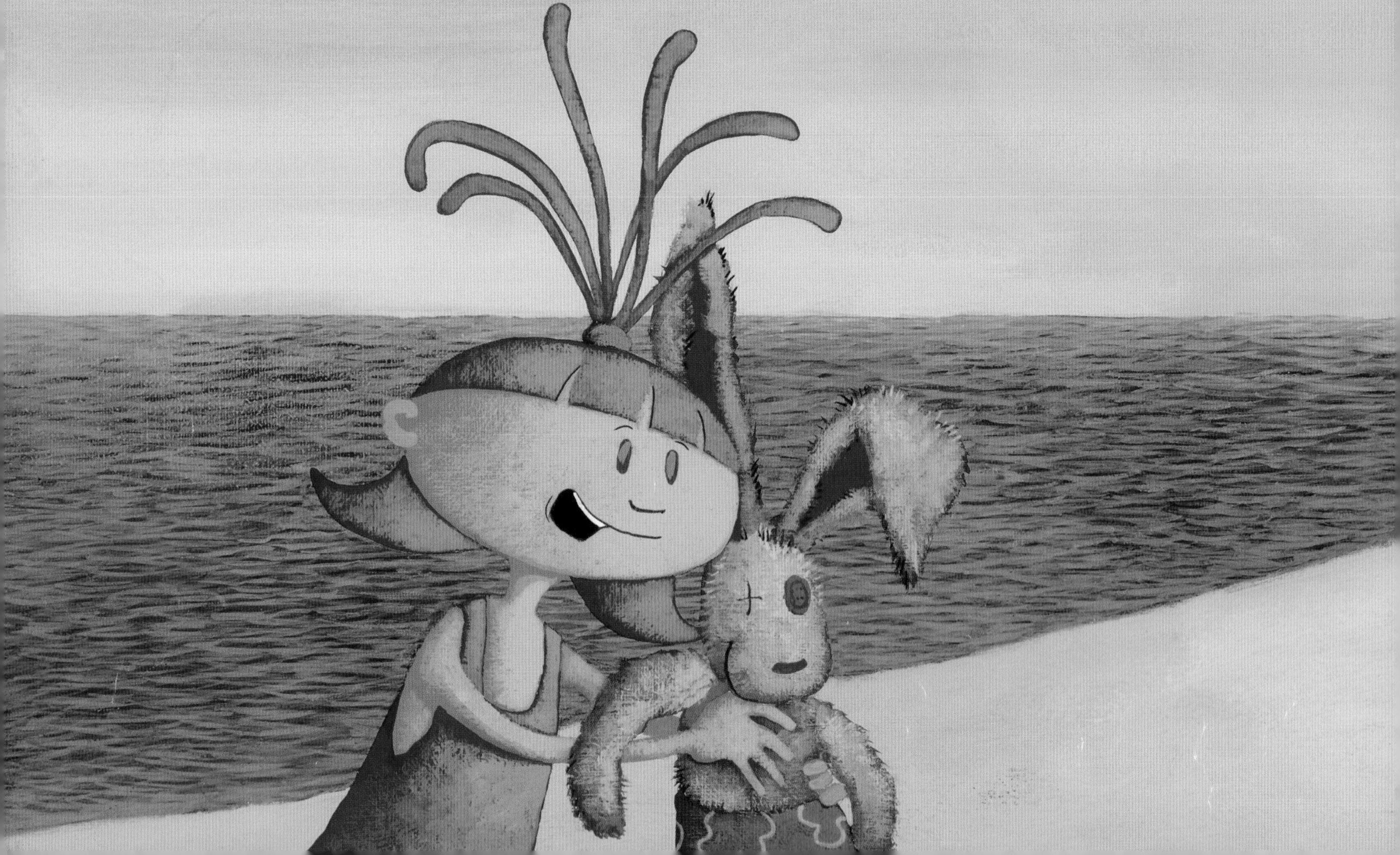

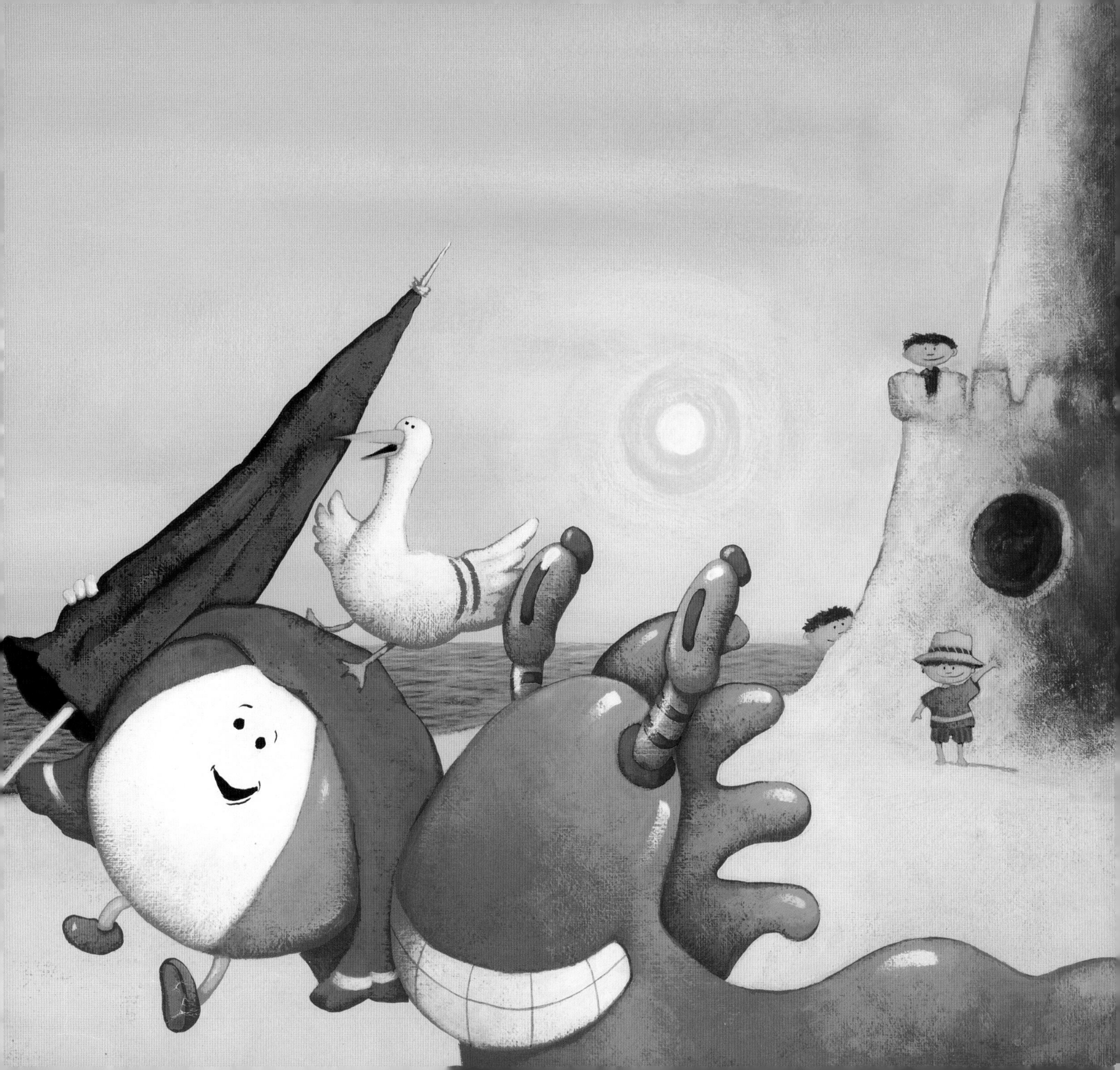

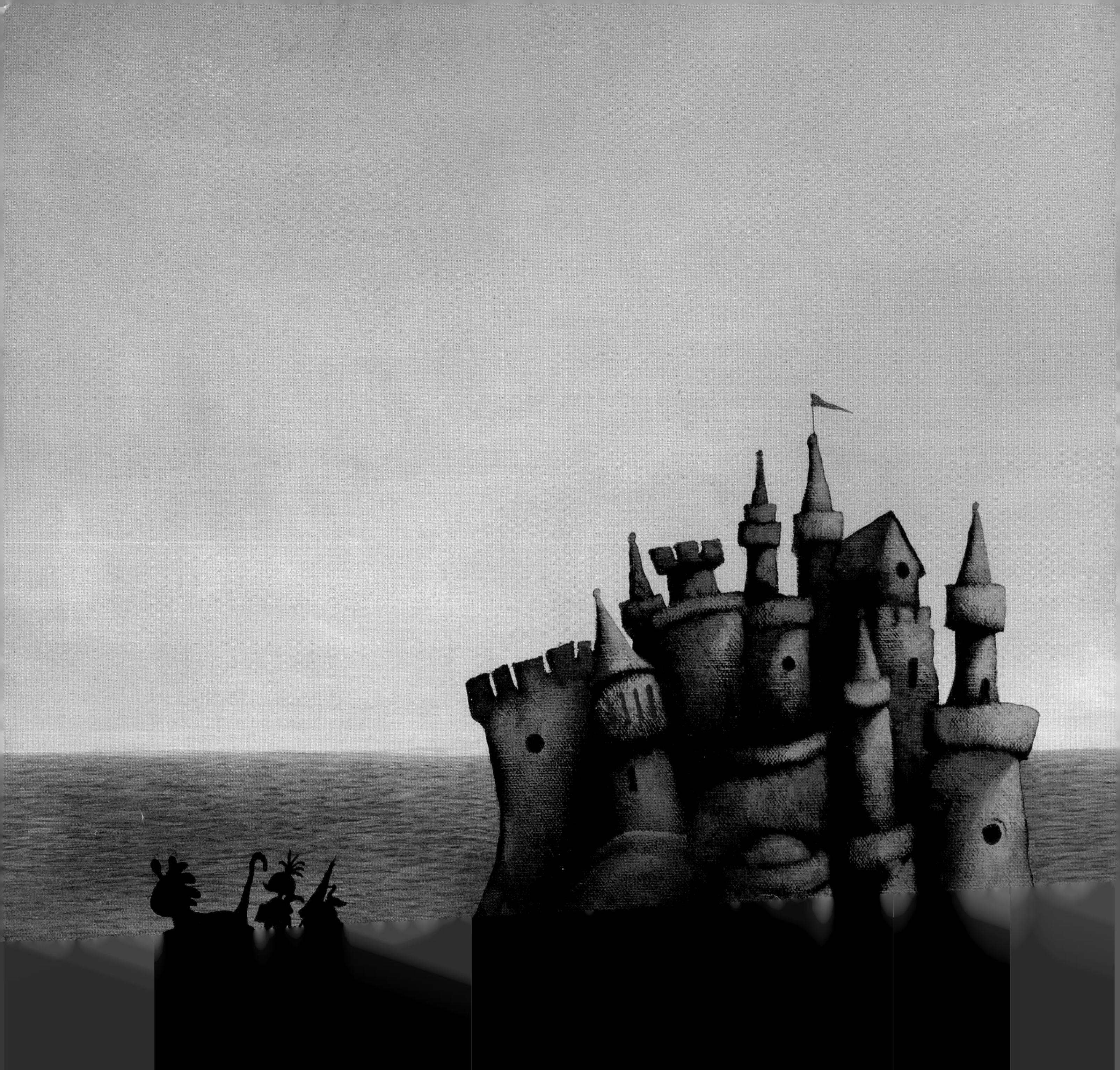

"We'll build a **rocket**," said Bob.

"And travel to the **stars**," said Rigby.

"We'll think of something spectacular," said Taffy. As the sun sank into the sea, they turned toward home.

Rollo laughed. "I hope it's not **windy** on the **moon**."

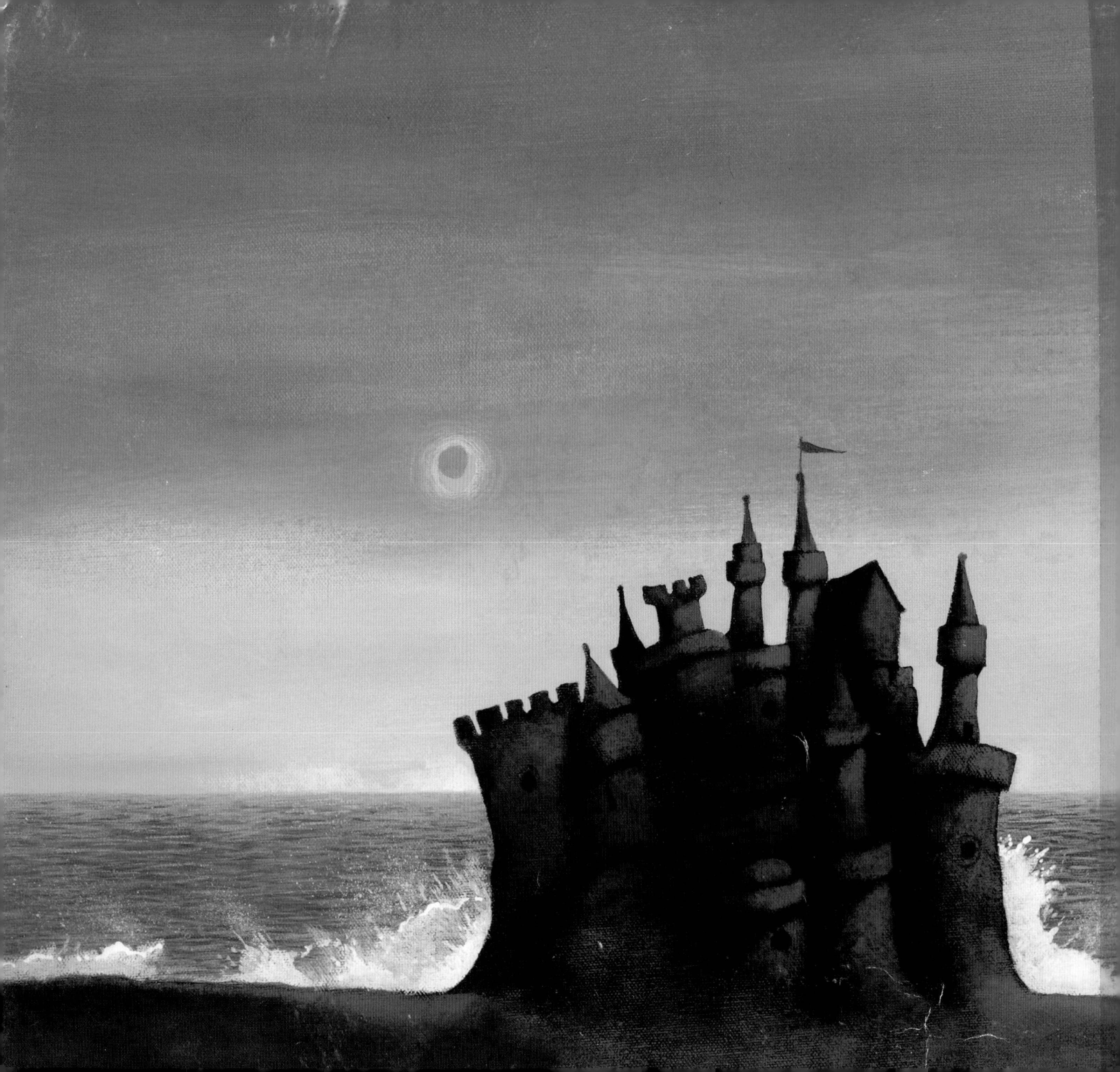